Farshore

First published in Great Britain 2021 by Farshore
An imprint of HarperCollins*Publishers*
1 London Bridge Street, London SE1 9GF

farshore.co.uk

HarperCollins*Publishers*
1st Floor, Watermarque Building, Ringsend Road
Dublin 4, Ireland

Text copyright © Annabelle Sami 2021
Illustration copyright © Allen Fatimaharan 2021
The moral rights of the author and illustrator have been asserted.

ISBN 978-1-4052-9755-4
Printed in Great Britain by CPI Group
1

Stay safe online. Any website addresses listed in this book are correct at the time
of going to print. However, Farshore is not responsible for content hosted by
third parties. Please be aware that online content can be subject to change
and websites can contain content that is unsuitable for children.
We advise that all children are supervised when using the internet.

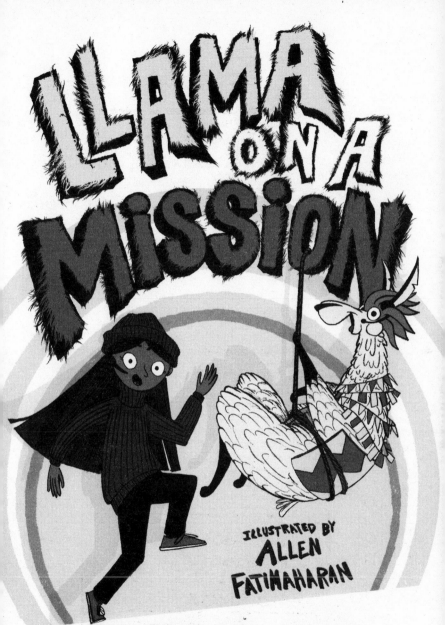

LLAMA ON A MISSION

ILLUSTRATED BY
ALLEN
FATIMAHARAN

ANNABELLE SAMI

This book is for the quiet ones.
I hope it makes you laugh, really, really loud.

CHAPTER ONE
The Facts

If you picked this book up expecting a sensible and serious story, then I must warn you now that you may be disappointed.

You see, 'sensible' and 'serious' are words that don't feature too heavily in this story. Along with words like 'respectable', 'scholarly' or 'mature and sophisticated'.

Here are some words you *will* find, however, and if they take your fancy, I suggest you read on:

- Llama (that's definitely in there)
- Lasers
- Loudmouth
- London

There are other words that don't begin with an L too, I promise.

Now that you're sure you want to go ahead with this story, there are two important facts we should go over first. This is the second story in Yasmin and Levi's adventure. If you wanted to, you could put this book down, go and read the first one and then come back to avoid those dreaded *spoilers*. But you don't have to; I can't tell you what to do.

Okay, Fact One: Levi is a magical llama. He's loud and annoying but means well. Oh, and did I mention he's part of a secret organisation of guardian llamas called Seen Not Herd who help children? Yep. He used to be undercover as a toy but after a run-in with his boss he got turned back into a real llama and slammed up in the City Farm. Bummer.

Fact Two: Yasmin is a ten-year-old girl with a huge noisy family. In fact, they are so noisy that for the last seven years of her life she decided not to speak. At all. It was only after she made a wish – 'I

3

wish I could stand up for myself.' – that Levi came into her life and helped her find her voice. (By 'helped' I mean he annoyed her so much she eventually had to speak to shut him up.)

At first Yasmin couldn't stand Levi. His antics got her into a lot of trouble. But once she realised he was only trying to help, his irritating presence became a bit easier to bear. He helped her stand up to her prankster brothers, her overbearing aunties and her loud parents.

Anyway, enough about the past. It's Yasmin's first day of Year Six at Fish Lane Primary School and her tummy has got enough butterflies to open a zoo or at least some kind of botanical garden. None of the other kids have heard Yasmin speak since a little incident where she mixed up her words and ended up shouting 'Poo' in assembly. It's quite hard to come back from *that* . . .

Luckily, she has a new friend, her only friend at school: Ezra.

She wouldn't be going into Year Six alone.

She had Ezra and a magical talking llama by her side.

AND she could speak now.

What could possibly go wrong?

CHAPTER TWO
First Day Jitters

'And remember when my skateboard went whoooooooshhh up into the air but I still managed to get my feet back on the board and flip it over and I stuck the landing?' Ezra acted out all the motions of his heroic feat while they made their way down Brick Lane towards school. It was 8.20am and Yasmin was nervous but excited. Ezra seemed to have all the energy in the world, recalling the tricks he'd managed to learn over the summer holidays.

'Mm-hmm,' Yasmin murmured in agreement. 'That was cool.'

'Summer was *great* . . . Even though you were "visiting your Aunt Gail" all the time.' Ezra said this in air quotes and gave Yasmin a suspicious look.

She laughed awkwardly and shrugged it off.

Yasmin had split her time that summer between playing checkers at the Octogenarians' London Daycentre (OLD), hanging out with Ezra and visiting Levi at the City Farm. Ezra liked to come and play at the City Farm too, but little did he know that the Llama he called Buttercup was actually a magical undercover guardian llama. It could get quite stressful for Yasmin being able to hear Levi blabbering away while all Ezra saw was a normal llama munching grass. So she'd started to visit Levi alone and hangout with Ezra at the skatepark separately. She'd had to make up a few excuses about why she couldn't hang out with Ezra on the days when she saw Levi, like her pretend Aunt Gail.

Of course, it didn't make her feel good to have to lie to him, but what could she do? Levi and the whole SNH organisation was top secret. To make up for the excuses, Yasmin would go round to Ezra's to play on his new set of drums. They'd had loads of fun trying to recreate the theme tune to their favourite TV soap show, though Yasmin wasn't sure if the neighbours liked it so much.

But the absolute best part of summer for Yasmin was the new comic she'd been working on, which she was calling *LOUDMOUTH*. Using her real-life experience, the story was about a girl called Jasmine and her talking toy alpaca sidekick, Leroy. Though, of course, anyone reading it would think it was just

make-believe. Yasmin had hours of fun scribbling away in her attic room as the summer sun set late into the evening. Art had always been an escape for her, from family drama and the difficulties of school. When she was drawing everything else melted away and she was totally in the world of the picture. That was magic.

Thinking back to her summer memories gave Yasmin a boost as they neared the school gates. She'd always had trouble at school. After all, it was hard to make friends and make yourself known when you don't speak. But now that she had the confidence to speak again thanks to Levi, plus her own best friend, Ezra, Yasmin felt like everything would be different. She'd tried to picture herself in class, chatting with the other kids, cracking jokes, even putting her hand up to answer questions from teachers.

'Now that I'm speaking, everything will be easier,' Yasmin assured herself. 'Won't it?'

'Come on, Yas. Don't worry too much.' Ezra patted her on the shoulder. 'I'm sure no one will even notice you're talking now!'

Yasmin took a deep breath. 'Maybe you're right. I'll probably just blend right in with everyone else. I mean, everyone speaks, so what's the big deal?'

Ezra grabbed the sleeve of her school jumper

and dragged her along behind him, making her giggle. Yep, she'd be a normal kid now like everyone else.

'Oh. Em. Gee. Yasmin's TALKING! Everybody, come listen!!!' Tia screeched.

Immediately after Yasmin had opened her mouth to talk to Ezra in registration period Tia had come running over. Yasmin and Tia didn't have the best history, with Tia having branded her as 'weird' for deciding not to speak when they were in Year Three. Now she was acting like the sky had fallen down because Yasmin had uttered a sentence.

'Say something again. Go on,' Tia sniggered, while the rest of Class 6A gathered round.

Yasmin felt her cheeks going bright red and she attempted to sink down into her chair and hide away.

'Leave her alone.' Ezra batted away the prying

eyes. 'She doesn't have to speak if she doesn't feel like it.'

Where was Miss Zainab when you needed her? Yasmin looked at the door, willing her teacher to walk in and save her from having to perform like a dancing monkey for her classmates.

Tia prodded her on the arm. 'Just do it, Yasmin! Come on! Say the two times table or something.'

'Well, I wouldn't want to confuse you, Tia,' Yasmin blurted out.

The group surrounding her went quiet. *Uh-oh.* Yasmin had meant to say that in her head like she used to. But now that she could speak . . . it sort of just came out.

A few boys giggled, which made Tia's face flush an even deeper shade of red than Yasmin's.

'Rude,' Tia announced, before heading back to her desk, her posse of friends following her.

Well . . . that definitely wasn't the triumphant return to school that Yasmin had planned.

Ezra turned to Yasmin wide-eyed, but before he could say anything Miss Zainab came bustling into the room, clutching a pile of papers.

'Good morning, Class 6A. First day of Year Six, isn't this exciting?'

Yasmin thought Miss Zainab's face looked more stressed than excited but kept her thoughts to herself this time.

'I've got your after-school activity forms here. You each have to choose at least one. Fill them out now, but remember we need your parents to sign the bottom of the form. The activities will begin next week.'

Miss Zainab began handing out the forms and the class excitedly chatted about their choices. Some of the boys at the back of the class were already on the football team, so it was obvious what they'd pick. There were also options for French-speaking club, athletics, a ukulele band and the debate team, but Yasmin knew exactly what she was going to pick

– she'd been thinking about it all summer.

She turned to Ezra with a sparkle in her eye. 'I can't wait to do art club. In Year Six you get to use the watercolour paints. Plus Ms Woods always brings in cakes for everyone and she said I was talented at landscapes last term.'

'Cakes do sound good . . .' Ezra was chewing on his pencil, mulling over his choices in his mind. 'But obviously I'm going to do music club. They need my mad drumming skills.' Ezra put a big tick next to music club on his form. 'But have fun in doodle club,' he said, winking.

Yasmin pushed him playfully. 'I *will*. I'm going to use the time to work on my *LOUDMOUTH* comic so I can enter it into this.' Yasmin carefully checked that Miss Zainab was absorbed in helping students fill out their forms before she reached into her rucksack. Then she pulled out her favourite magazine, *Comic Action*, and flipped open the back page.

Yasmin smiled at the page, thinking of what it would be like to have her work looked at by a real comic book artist. Then she put a big tick next to the option of art club on her form.

Miss Zainab circled over to Yasmin and Ezra's table, leaving the other students chatting about their choices.

'So, Ezra, you've chosen music club, no surprise there. Mr J has told me how much you love the drums.'

'Yep. It's been helping me focus!' Ezra did a little

15

drum on the table using a pen and pencil. Ezra had ADHD so Mr J was a special teacher who gave him extra help in lessons sometimes.

Then Miss Zainab turned to Yasmin, a smile on her face. 'Now, Yasmin, I have something very exciting to tell you.'

'Okay,' Yasmin replied.

Miss Zainab yelped, making the whole class look up. 'Nothing to worry about, everyone; go back to your work.' Miss Zainab stared at Yasmin wide-eyed. 'Yasmin, you're speaking now?'

'Yes.'

Miss Zainab straightened her headscarf. 'Right, well, brilliant! That will make what I'm about to tell you even better.'

Ezra and Yasmin leaned forward in their seats. It was only the first day of term – what exciting news could Miss Zainab have?

'Yasmin, I've selected you to join our competitive science team, the Funsen Burners!'

Miss Zainab beamed at Yasmin. Yasmin blinked back at Miss Zainab.

'Funsen . . . like, a Bunsen burner? Okay, the name is a work in progress, but aren't you pleased? After your brilliant score in the end-of-year tests I just knew we had to have you on the team.

We'll compete against another school in various science experiments and there will be quizzes and a trophy! It's going to be so much fun.'

Miss Zainab finally stopped to breathe and looked at Yasmin expectedly. But Yasmin was looking down at her activity form. The science team was after school on a Tuesday, the same time as art club. Once her parents found out she'd been selected for the science team, there's no way they'd let her do art club . . .

'There are only three of you on the team. So I can count you in, yes?' Miss Zainab tapped the form on Yasmin's table, then hurried off to her desk.

'I – I, um, guess . . .' Yasmin stammered, unable to get her words out.

'But what about art club?' Ezra was still drumming on the table, but he stopped when he saw the smile drop from Yasmin's face.

'My parents are always keeping track of my academic record. My dad is convinced that one day

I'll study biology like he did. There's no way they'll let me skip science team for art club.' Yasmin bit her lip so that it wouldn't wobble. In her mind she could see watercolours, cake and comics melting away . . .

'But maybe if you explained to them?' Ezra offered. 'My parents were really happy when they saw how much I liked the drums!'

'My parents are different,' Yasmin snapped, a twinge of jealousy growing in her chest. But Ezra was only trying to help. 'Sorry, Ezra. They just don't listen to me when it comes to stuff about school.'

Ezra sighed. 'That's rubbish, Yasmin. Sorry.'

This wasn't how Yasmin had imagined her first day back at all. Weren't things supposed to be easier now she was talking?

Then the bell rang, so Yasmin merely shrugged and tried to hide her disappointment. She put a tick next to 'science team' and a thick black line through 'art club'.

If there was one person (or animal) that knew just how bossy Yasmin's parents could be, it was Levi. So after school Yasmin found herself walking the opposite way home, heading down the road towards City Farm with a determined step. She needed someone to rant to and if there was one thing Levi *loved*, it was drama.

She stomped all the way down Brick Lane, across the mini roundabout and crawled through the hole in the bushes that she still considered her secret entrance to the farm. By now the farm staff knew her pretty well, considering she had spent so much time there over the summer talking to 'Buttercup' the llama. As she emerged on the other side of the bush and on to the dirt track by the chicken pens,

Ronaldo the farm hand spotted her.

'Yasmin, *hola*! Buttercup is in the shed; he's being very naughty today . . .' Ronaldo showed her a tear in his T-shirt, no doubt from a certain naughty llama's wonky teeth.

'Okay, Ronaldo, I'll be careful,' she called back to him, shaking her head.

Levi had certainly made a name for himself here at the farm since he had been suddenly 'shipped in overnight from a llama sanctuary' earlier in the summer. As Yasmin made her way to his shed, she found herself puzzling once again how a secret organisation of toy llamas managed to operate undetected in a city like London. 'Buttercup' being shipped from a llama sanctuary was a clever cover story orchestrated by them. A few times she'd woken up in the middle of the night and wondered if it was all a dream. But, nope, Seen Not Herd definitely existed and the boss of the whole organisation, Mama Llama, was *really angry* with

Levi for telling Yasmin about them. So angry that she'd turned Levi from a stinky, grubby toy llama into the stinky, grubby *real* llama Yasmin saw in front of her now.

'Yassy!' came the familiar cockney voice, as he stuck his neck over the stable door of his shed. 'How was ya first day? Still the class weirdo?'

'Still the farm pain in the bum?' Yasmin retorted, sticking her tongue out.

'Ugh, I gotta get out of here, Yassy.' Levi scuffed a foot against the ground. 'It's so boring and that farm hand better not try and feed me any more of that dry, stale hay if he wants to keep the rest of his T-shirt.'

Yasmin felt a hint of guilt. Levi had been turned into a real llama and trapped here after she'd texted Mama Llama about how rubbish he was as a guardian.

'I'm sorry, Levi.' She reached out and patted his rough furry head.

Levi softened. 'Nah, don't you fret. If I weren't so rubbish at helping you find yer voice, you wouldn't have had to snitch on me.'

'I wasn't a snitch!'

Levi winked. He was far too good at winding Yasmin up. 'I've tried to liven the place up a little bit anyway. I forced the other llamas to do karaoke with me and I started making a hammock out of hay, though it fell apart . . . I even put that poster up.'

Yasmin looked into the shed where a poster of a cat holding on to a branch of a tree said 'Hang in there!'.

'But nothing works. This lot are booooorrrinnnggg.'

The two other llamas were huddled in the shed, their legs curled up underneath them, doing their best to ignore Levi, who was now doing a funny dance in front of them to try and get a reaction.

'What about Mama Llama? Has she told you when she might turn you back into a

24

toy again or will you be here forever?' Yasmin asked quietly. She knew the farm staff already thought she was a bit weird after they'd caught her talking to a llama a few times, but they didn't need to know about Seen Not Herd.

Levi huffed, trotting out of the shed and plonking himself down on the grass. 'Not a clue, love. But tell me 'bout school. What did the kids think about your trombone voice?'

Yasmin frowned. Her voice was indeed quite low and booming, but she didn't appreciate the nickname her brothers had given her. Levi, on the other hand, was quite fond of it.

'Tia thought it was weird. Miss Zainab's eyes basically popped out her head when I spoke to her. Plus, she wants me to join the science team, the "Funsen Burners".'

'Stupid name.'

'I know! I really wanted to do art club, but they're at the same time and you know what my parents are like about academic stuff.' Yasmin sighed and leaned against the stable door. 'But I've been looking forward to art club since, like, Year Three.'

Levi scratched his belly with one of his back legs. 'Just tell 'em you wanna do art. Sometimes you just gotta stick it to them.'

Yasmin put her hands on her hips and gave the llama an unimpressed look. 'You really think it's that easy? Look how long it took me to even be able to speak to them! They still don't listen. I thought being able to talk was going to make everything easier . . .'

Levi sighed. 'Maybe you're right, Yassy. What do I know, hey? I'm just a failed guardian llama stuck in a paddock, eating grass all day.' For extra dramatic effect Levi flung his long neck to the ground and buried his face in the grass.

It seemed like both of them were at a dead end. But in the distance, by the trees next to the enclosure, something caught Yasmin's eye. A glinting light at the top of the trees. But now it was falling gently. It looked like a small balloon made of shiny material . . . and there was something hanging from it!

'Psst, Levi! Look there!' Yasmin whispered urgently, pointing in the direction of the strange object.

'Not now, Yasmin. I'm having a moment,' Levi groaned, still face down in the grass.

'Seriously, Levi. Look! There's something coming this way.'

Levi languidly lifted his long neck and craned it round in the direction of the trees. But once he spotted what Yasmin had pointed at, his ears pricked up and his whole body went stiff.

'Quick, Yasmin. Hide behind the food trough,' he whispered, getting up on to all four legs.

'Why? What is it?' she replied, crouching down behind the large metal basin.

'It's Seen Not Herd. They've sent someone.'

CHAPTER FOUR
The Name's Travis, Agent Travis

Yasmin knelt down behind the feeding trough of the llama shed, far too close for comfort to a pile of dung. Someone ... or some llama ... was coming to see Levi. Could it be that Mama Llama had changed her mind and Levi could be a toy llama again? Or was she coming to announce he would be this way ... forever?

Peeking through a gap in between the food and water troughs, Yasmin could just about make out the figure of a small llama-shaped object whizzing through the grass in the paddock. How was it moving so quickly? Yasmin peered as far as she could through the gap, without actually putting her face in the soggy hay, until she could finally see what it was. A toy llama for sure ... but it was riding an electric scooter! Attached to the llama's back was a small rucksack from which a shiny parachute was dragging behind it.

So that's what she had seen glinting in the sky! The llama had parachuted down into the paddock.

The low buzz of the tiny electric scooter whirred past the farm door where Levi still stood and into the shed. No! Now Yasmin couldn't see a thing. She jumped to her feet and, checking around her to see she wasn't being watched, slunk round to the back of the shed next to some bushes. There was a gap in between the slats that allowed her to see Levi, the small toy llama on the scooter and the two other City Farm llamas, all eyeing each other up.

The toy llama hopped off its scooter, folding it up with a flick of its leg. Yasmin suppressed a giggle, after all, this was a very serious moment – Levi's fate might be in this toy llama's hands! (Well, technically llamas, including toy llamas, only have feet but you catch my drift.)

The toy llama stepped towards Levi. 'We need to speak. Alone.'

Levi looked over at his City Farm paddock mates. 'Oi, Daisy, Marigold. Give us a minute. This won't take long.'

Daisy and Marigold heaved themselves up on to their legs and sauntered out of the shed, happy to leave the llama-drama behind them. Levi and whoever this toy llama was clearly didn't like each other.

Levi narrowed his eyes. 'What do you want, Travis?'

Travis was standing in the light now and Yasmin could make out his chocolate-brown shiny fur, plus the long hair on his head that was styled into a quiff. Travis meant business.

'I've been sent here by Mama Llama herself. If it were up to me, I'd leave you here, but she wants to give you once last chance.'

Yasmin bit her lip. Yikes. This guy really did not rate Levi at all.

'Great, bring it on. I'm ready.' Levi puffed out his chest and lifted his head high, accidentally bumping it on the beam above him. 'Ow!'

'Riiight.' Travis looked distinctly unimpressed. 'You'll be assigned one final mission. Mama Llama herself is on her way from Peru right now to supervise you. Complete the mission and you'll be allowed to return to toy-llama form as a free Seen Not Herd operative.'

'And if I don't complete it?' Levi asked in a quieter voice.

Travis smirked and flicked the quiff back from his face. 'You'll be sent back to Peru to live the rest of your life as a real farmyard llama.'

Yasmin's stomach dropped. As much as Levi had been a pain, she couldn't lose him.

Travis unclipped his electric scooter and kicked it round perfectly to land under his feet. From some unknown pocket he'd now produced a pair of sunglasses, which he stylishly perched on his long nose. 'You'll be turned back into a toy llama tonight under the full moon. The mission will be assigned afterwards. You know the ritual . . . make sure you're alone.'

With those final words, Travis knocked his scooter back into gear and whizzed out of the shed and into the far trees where he'd landed. As soon as he was out of earshot, Levi blew a huge raspberry at his back.

Yasmin rushed back round to the front of the shed. 'WHO was that?'

Levi scoffed. 'Ugh . . . Travis. He's the head of the London paddock. Show-off.'

Yasmin screwed up her face in confusion. 'London paddock?'

'Every country in the world has a Seen Not Herd HQ; it's called a paddock. Actually ... there isn't one on Easter Island; we haven't figured out how to get there yet. Anyway, Travis is the boss of the UK paddock.' Levi was pacing around the small shed as he relayed this information. He seemed on edge.

'But this is good news, right? You're going to be turned back into a toy again.' Yasmin tried to make her voice sound hopeful, but she was worried too. Levi hadn't exactly excelled in his last mission to help her ... 'What did he say about a ritual?'

Levi's eyes widened. 'Wait ... you could hear him?'

Yasmin nodded.

'That don't make no sense. You can hear me cos I'm your guardian llama. But Travis too?' Now Levi was really pacing.

'Can I watch you turn back into a toy?' Yasmin was intrigued now. I mean, a talking toy llama was obviously magic but to actually see it *happen*? That would be cool.

But Levi shook his head. 'Na-uh, no chance. That's sacred llama magic. For llamas only.'

Yasmin shrugged. This was all getting *very* complicated and very strange. She wished more than anything she could share this with Ezra. But Levi had told her that would go against all the rules in the Seen Not Herd rule book.

'Look, love. I'm gonna be turned into a toy again under the full moon. Go home and wait for me there. Leave your window open. We'll rendezvous at midnight.'

Yasmin had never seen Levi so serious. He was talking like a secret agent or something. Usually he just gossiped about the other farm animals or made fart jokes. Sensing that something very important was about to happen, Yasmin gave him one last pat on the head. 'I'll see you later?'

Levi smiled a big real-llama smile. 'See you later.'

CHAPTER FIVE
A New Mission

Yasmin took her time walking back home, aware that as soon as she showed her parents the activity sheet, her fate in the Funsen Burners would be sealed. It was a dreary September afternoon and the light rain had settled into a steady stream by the time Yasmin got to the front door. It was only the coldness of her soggy school jumper that gave her the motivation to open the front door of her tall thin house and step inside.

A tsunami of sound (a sound-nami) hit Yasmin bang in the face as she entered the kitchen. Shouted conversations, hissing pots of rice and daal, plus the blaring wall-mounted TV made it practically impossible to hear herself think. Ammi and Papa were sitting at the kitchen table discussing the news. Well, they called it discussing, but really they both simultaneously shouted their opinions at each other until one of them stopped for a sip of chai.

'YASMINDARLINGHOWWASSCHOOL?' Ammi bellowed in her usual fast and loud 'inside voice'.

'It was fine, I suppose.' Yasmin pulled up a chair and plonked her school bag down on the table.

'Just fine?' Papa seemed concerned. 'You mean you didn't do well in one of the classes?'

'BADMARKONASPELLINGTEST?' Ammi suggested.

'No, no, no.' Yasmin sighed and fished around in her bag for the activity sheet. 'Actually . . . Miss Zainab chose me for the science team.'

There was a brief respite in sound as Ammi wordlessly switched off the TV.

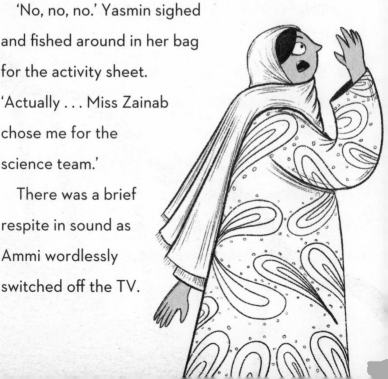

'SISTERSGUESSWHAT?' Ammi yelled in the direction of the stairs. Yasmin's twin aunties lived in the room above the kitchen and absolutely loved showing off about their nieces and nephews. This could only be bad news.

'WHAT?' came Auntie Gigi's voice in reply.

'YASMINHASBEENSELECTEDFORTHE SCIENCETEAM!'

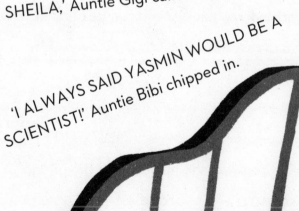

'OH, AMAZING! I MUST TELL AUNTIE SHEILA,' Auntie Gigi called back.

'I ALWAYS SAID YASMIN WOULD BE A SCIENTIST!' Auntie Bibi chipped in.

Papa was beaming from ear to ear, his moustache perched high up on his top lip. 'My daughter . . . *specially chosen* for the science team . . . from hundreds of candidates!'

'Well . . . it was only my class, Papa–'

But Yasmin's words fell on deaf ears as Ammi's phone started ringing.

'HELLO? OHH, NASREEN, HI. YES, SHE WAS CHOSEN AS HEAD OF THE SCIENCE TEAM . . .'

What? This news was spreading too fast. And Ammi's friend Nasreen lived in Lahore! How had she found out so quickly? Yasmin put her head in her hands. Trust her family to blow everything out of proportion.

She felt Ammi put a hand on her shoulder and she looked up. Ammi's smile was huge and her eyes were full of pride as she nattered on the phone.

Her parents were proud of her and she'd made them happy. As a daughter, wasn't that what she was meant to do? There was no way she was going to bring up art club now.

Yasmin left the activity letter on the table for Papa to sign and headed up to her room. Her house, 11 Fish Lane, was squished in between the two houses next to it, so there was only space for one room on each floor. Yasmin had the attic room right at the top of the house, so now she started the long journey up the central staircase that passed through each bedroom in turn.

First she passed through the aunties' bright-pink bedroom, filled with rose-coloured velvet furniture and matching beds. They were both individually on the phone to another auntie, still singing Yasmin's praises. In the space of five minutes they'd probably notified a whole village that Yasmin had won the Nobel Prize. Auntie Gigi briefly met Yasmin's eye and gave her a big thumbs up, but they were both so engrossed in their conversations that Yasmin could nip up the stairs quickly without too much attention.

The next room was Ammi and Papa's, which

always smelled like Ammi's jasmine perfume and moth balls. Even though it was a strange combination, Yasmin always felt comforted when she smelled it on her parents' clothes.

The room above her parents' room belonged to her two brothers. Yasmin had her own nicknames for them: Tall Brother and Short Brother. To say they were the biggest pain in the bum of her life might be an exaggeration – they were more like a mosquito bite. Itchy, annoying and always popping up when you least wanted them too.

Luckily for Yasmin her brothers had been banished to stay with Daadi, their grandma, in Pakistan for the summer. She was the strictest and most fearsome lady in the northern hemisphere. Usually her brothers would plan a horrible prank every time Yasmin came home from school, but with them gone for another week she was safe for a while.

She crossed through their room, which was the tidiest and nicest it had smelled in forever, and walked up the stairs to her attic bedroom. The first thing she noticed was a letter on the bed, which was addressed to her in her brother's handwriting. Daadi had been making them send regular correspondence so that wasn't that surprising.

She picked up the letter, unfolded the envelope and out dropped – a huge black spider!!!

'ARGH!' Yasmin screamed, frantically swiping it off her jumper before it fell to the floor motionless. It was made of rubber. So now her brothers were pulling off pranks from the other side of the world?!

Dear Yasmin,

HA! Got you! We wish we could have seen your face when you opened this. Bet it was priceless. See you next week, so watch out.

From Hamza and Tariq

P.S. Hope you had a good first day back. Have the other kids worked out how weird you are yet?

So her parents and aunties thought she was a science prodigy and her brothers thought she was a loser. When all she actually wanted to be was an artist. Or to at least go to art club.

Yasmin opened the drawer in her bedside table and got out her *LOUDMOUTH* comic. There wasn't much room in her bedroom, but her papa had managed to fit in a single bed, a small wardrobe and a desk for Yasmin to do her homework at. But Yasmin had filled every inch of the walls with her drawings and above her bed, her pride and joy, was a huge chalkboard wall. Yasmin sat down at her 'homework desk', which was covered in coloured pens, pencils and special fine liners bought with her allowance. She got out her comic and looked at the cover, which she'd spent so long perfecting.

Maybe if she tried really hard and won the comic book competition in *Comic Action* her parents would be just as proud as they were of her science team place. If she could win, her parents might take

her art seriously and realise that she was talented in that too ... But she'd have to finish the comic first.

After Yasmin had been down for dinner and endured yet more science team exaggerations, she headed back to her bedroom and lay down on her bed. There was a lot to think about and it was hard to sort through on her own. She decided to ring her friend Gilly – one of the members at OLD.

Back when Yasmin was still as silent as a mouse,

she'd been going to OLD as part of a school programme. OLD was a daycentre for people aged eighty and above where they could go, hang out and gossip about things that annoyed them. Yasmin's school programme mostly involved playing checkers and listening to Gilly's crazy stories – she was quite adventurous. But even when the school programme had ended and Yasmin had found her voice, she and Gilly had stayed firm friends. In fact, Yasmin and Ezra had even been invited to her eighty-fifth birthday party over the summer. They went go-karting at Wacky Races Motor Rink. Gilly won obviously.

'Hiya, Yasmin. I'm still not used to you calling me.' Gilly was normally a text kind of person, as was Yasmin before she had started speaking.

'Yeah, it's a bit weird for me too. But I need your advice.'

'Well then, I'm all ears. As soon as I turn my hearing aid on.' Gilly laughed at her own joke and

Yasmin instantly felt more at ease. She told Gilly all about the comic competition, art club and being chosen for the science team.

'But my mum and dad think science and maths are the most important things in the world. There's no way I can convince them!' Yasmin huffed, finally finishing her rant. It felt surprisingly good to get everything off her chest but also a little strange. After all, she used to never say *anything* so all those words had just stayed stuck in her throat.

'Well, Yasmin, that really is a pickle.' Gilly sighed. 'But I think you've got a good plan there with finishing your comic. I don't know any parent who doesn't love the pictures their kids draw – even when they're rubbish. Not that your drawings are rubbish.'

Yasmin giggled. 'Okay, so I should finish my comic and then try to use that to convince them to let me do art club?'

Gilly was quiet for a moment. 'Just focus on your

comics. That's what you love, so that's what is important.'

Yasmin thanked Gilly and said goodbye. Talking about her science-team conundrum had helped, but there was still something weighing heavily on Yasmin's shoulders. A big prob-llama.

Levi was on thin ice with Mama Llama and one last mission could either save him or seal his fate forever. Yasmin couldn't imagine life without him now. She wondered whether she'd still have the confidence to speak without him around. It all seemed very confusing. If only she could talk *this* through with Gilly . . . or Ezra . . . or anyone for that matter! But it was one big secret she had to keep to herself.

After working on her comic for a while, Yasmin felt the familiar ease and comfort that drawing brought her and it settled her thoughts. She'd managed to map out a whole page of comic panels and by the time she put her pens away she was smiling again.

She changed into her PJs and opened her window, letting the cool night air in. Then she crawled into bed but left her bedside lamp on. It was 9.30pm now, so she could definitely stay awake until midnight when Levi's transformation took place . . . that was only two and a half hours. Maybe she could daydream . . . or draw . . . or . . . .

Yasmin bolted upright, her eyes adjusting to the darkness. No! She had fallen asleep! Ammi must have come in and switched the light off. Yasmin felt around in the dark on her bedside table for her phone. The screen said: 12.15.

Where was Levi?

Had the spell not worked? Or maybe he had tried to find her house but couldn't remember where it was? A thousand thoughts flitted about in Yasmin's head before she realised she could hear a faint noise outside her window. It seemed to be getting louder, as if whatever was making the sound was getting closer.

Sitting up in bed, Yasmin lifted her head so she could peer out the window at the street below. But she could see nothing there apart from some neighbourhood cats and a raggedy fox having a stand-off. Where was Levi?!

A sound brought Yasmin's attention to the rooftops of the houses opposite. Then she saw it. A pigeon flying directly towards her, making a noise that sounded like,

WahoooooooooooooooooooooooOOO!

But, as the pigeon flew closer, she realised it wasn't making the sound at all. It was Levi flying in on the pigeon's back like he was wrangling a dragon. The pigeon swooped on to her window ledge and bowed its head.

'Levi! You're a toy again!' Yasmin jumped out of bed and ran over to the windowsill, picking up Levi.

'I sure am, love!' Levi hopped up and down on his little llama legs. 'And what an entrance, right? Thought you'd like that.'

Levi nodded at the pigeon and it flew off into the night, leaving a single feather behind on the window ledge.

'I tried to get one of them parachutes Travis had, but they said it's just for the high-ranking agents,' Levi grumbled.

'So you're a guardian llama again?' Yasmin had so many questions, but most of all, she wanted to know that Levi would be sticking around for a while.

'Yep. I've got to complete one more mission, though.' Levi smirked and jumped down on to Yasmin's bed, getting comfy. 'Guess what it is?'

'What?'

'No, I said "guess",' Levi huffed.

Yasmin didn't have time for this, it was 12.20pm and she had school in the morning, so she simply put her hands on her hips and stared Levi down.

'All right, fine.' Levi stood up on his back two legs and pulled a superhero pose. 'I'm gonna get you into art club.'

CHAPTER SIX
Secret Agent Levi

Now, I don't know how many of you have shared a bed with a magical toy llama, but they are NOT good sleepover mates. Yasmin discovered this the hard way after spending a week of sleepless nights getting kicked in the face as Levi wriggled around, trying to get comfortable. He also tended to snore extremely loudly, meaning by the time Yasmin got to sleep she'd be rudely awoken again by a snort. When her alarm went off on Tuesday morning Yasmin's head felt like a foggy mess.

'Morning, Yassy. Wow, another great night's sleep!' Levi got up and stretched his fluffy legs 'A nice bed like this beats that cold shed any day. What's for breakfast?'

Yasmin glared at him with weary red eyes and hid

her face under her pillow.

'Oof, you look rough. Did I snore again?' Levi asked somewhat sheepishly.

'Tonight you're sleeping under the laundry basket!' Yasmin huffed and hauled herself out of bed.

It was going to be a long day.

By the time first break rolled round Yasmin felt like a sleep-deprived zombie, so it's fair to say she wasn't in the best mood. Not that Ezra picked up on this as he launched into a detailed explanation of how great music club had been the day before.

'And then I got to do a drum solo and I was like – ba-da-bum-dum-dum CRASH.' Ezra played an imaginary set of drums with Yasmin as the audience. 'The teacher said I was amazing at focusing and that next week we're going to learn a new song.'

Yasmin was pleased Ezra was finding it easier to concentrate. She was even happier that he loved the drums. But right then, in that moment, with minus-one hours of sleep and the first science-team practice looming, she didn't want to hear about how great Ezra's activity was.

'That's cool, Ezra,' she managed to say through a yawn.

'One more time with a bit more oomph!' Levi instructed, poking his head from behind a holly bush. Of course Levi had to come with her to school. Since getting this mission, Levi had decided to take his role as a Seen Not Herd operative *extremely* seriously, which was *extremely* annoying. He'd managed to find a tiny black suit from somewhere, which made him look like he was in *Men in Black*. He was monitoring Yasmin 'from a distance', meaning she'd spotted him lurking behind bins and bookcases all morning. He'd also been whispering into a concealed mouthpiece on his collar, even though Yasmin could see the wire wasn't connected to anything . . .

'It's cool you get to learn a new song!' Yasmin said

more brightly, following Levi's advice. But Ezra was looking at her strangely now.

'You seem tired all the time. And where have you been after school? I called at your house but your mum said you weren't there . . .' Ezra seemed a little hurt, but he was trying to play it cool. It gave Yasmin's heart a pang of guilt.

'Oh, I'm sorry. Yeah, it's just . . . I've been spending a lot of time with my aun–'

'Your Aunt Gail?' Ezra cut in. From the look on his face Yasmin knew he didn't believe her. But she couldn't tell him the truth – that she'd been preoccupied with a talking toy llama. Levi was coming between their friendship and she just hated it.

'Sorry, Ezra. Promise I'll come round soon.' Yasmin smiled but it seemed forced.

Ezra shrugged and the bell rang, marking the end of break.

Yawning again, Yasmin wondered how she would be able to make it to science-team practice after school without falling asleep on the test tubes. Miss Zainab told her in registration that morning that they were practising the experiment they'd be doing alongside another school next week. Even though Yasmin enjoyed science, doing it *instead* of art just made the whole thing seem like a chore. But she took a deep breath and tried to keep her chin up. She should be grateful . . . only three students had been chosen for the team. That was a compliment, right? Yasmin trudged back inside to the classroom with Ezra trailing glumly behind her for history. She looked over her shoulder to check if Levi was doing his 'following from a distance' thing, but he wasn't there.

'What are you looking for?' Ezra asked, following Yasmin's eyeline.

'Uh, nothing . . . I'm sure it's fine,' Yasmin replied, annoyed that once again she was lying to her friend. But if Levi had snuck off somewhere, that could only be a bad thing.

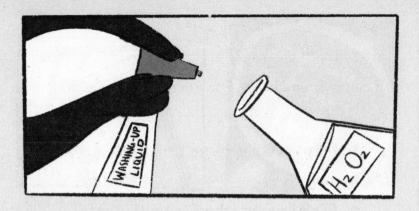

A quick note for you, sweet readers. Don't mess around with chemicals in the science lab. *Trust me.* It can only end badly. For example, you could:

1. **Burn your eyebrows off with a Bunsen burner.**
2. **Explode your school to smithereens.**
3. **Create a gas so stinky you will always smell it up your nose, even when it's gone, for the rest of time.**

Levi is a trained professional agent llama and, as such, has extensive training in dealing with chemicals. Even if he does mainly use that training to make stink bombs that he releases at the public swimming pool . . .

CHAPTER SEVEN
Yasmin the Science
Superhero

It was 3.30pm on Tuesday afternoon and the halls of Fish Lane Primary School were empty (apart from the few teachers who always stayed so late that Yasmin wondered if they lived there). As she trudged down the hall towards the science lab Yasmin heard a scurrying sound in the corridor behind her.

'Levi, just come out for goodness' sake. I know you're there.'

Peeping out from behind a locker, Yasmin saw Levi's ears, then the tuft of his hair, his face and finally his whole body sliding out guiltily.

'You must have super-hearing or summink!' Levi shook his head and he trotted up behind her. 'I was being well sneaky.'

'Phsst. Says you. Are you coming into practice or not?' Yasmin scooped Levi up and popped him in her rucksack. Science team was going to be rubbish, but if Levi was there it might at least give her a few giggles.

'I'm coming. Actually I thought it might be good for you to have a word with Miss Zainab after . . .' Levi suggested. He was still trying to look professional with his earpiece connected to the mouthpiece on his collar, but being squashed inside a rucksack wasn't helping.

Yasmin raised an eyebrow. 'Why?'

'Well, I thought maybe you could have a chat and convince her that you ain't that good at science . . . then she might let you leave the team!'

Yasmin shook her head. 'That would be lying though, Levi. And Miss Zainab has seen all my test results; she knows that isn't true.'

'All right . . . we'll try something different,' Levi said quietly. 'So who's on this Boring Burners team anyway?'

Yasmin paused with her hand on the door handle. She hadn't really thought about that. A familiar uneasiness settled into her stomach as she pushed open the door.

'Ah, Yasmin, glad you're here. Now our team is complete!' Miss Zainab said, smiling, already decked out in her white lab coat.

To Yasmin's horror, standing behind the workbench next to Miss Zainab was Tia! Yasmin's jaw immediately clenched. Tia really did not like Yasmin and the feeling was mutual. And they had to be science-team partners!? Tia was scowling at Yasmin, apparently just as unimpressed with Miss Zainab's choice of team mate.

'Oh no, not her again!' Levi groaned, looking in Tia's direction. Levi had once spent a lesson hurling small projectiles, like checker pieces and a rubber at Tia's back after he saw her be rude to Yasmin. It was very immature (but also a *teeny-weeny* bit funny, though Yasmin would never admit that).

'So, Yasmin, you obviously know Tia.' Miss Zainab beckoned her forward and handed Yasmin a lab coat. 'But this is Remi. He's in 6B and he's very talented at biology.'

'I study frogs in my back garden!' Remi announced.

Miss Zainab smiled. 'Uh . . . wonderful!'

Yasmin knew Remi. There were two Year Six classes at Fish Lane Primary but their classes had once worked together on a big chemistry experiment. Yasmin had been paired with Remi and she remembered him being *very* serious about chemicals and doing everything exactly to the instructions. It seemed he'd now moved on to frogs.

Miss Zainab clapped her hands together enthusiastically. 'Let's get on with practising this experiment. We'll be carrying this out at the end of the week against the team from Oakmead School, so pay careful attention to the measurements.'

Miss Zainab set to work, bustling about with trays and beakers in front of the unlikely team mates. Tia was in the middle, with Remi and Yasmin either side taking notes, as Miss Zainab explained the intended reactions of the experiment. They were all decked out in goggles, white lab coats and gloves, despite the fact that the experiment was simply inflating a balloon using the chemical reaction of yeast . . . Yasmin couldn't help but think Miss Zainab was taking the science team a *little bit* too seriously.

'Okay, Tia, add one tablespoon of the yeast to the beaker of warm water and stir. This will activate the yeast so it starts to give off carbon dioxide.'

Miss Zainab started writing up the chemical compositions on the board for Remi and Yasmin to copy down, but as Tia held the beaker of water Yasmin noticed something peeling off the beaker. It looked like a label.

'Wait a second, Tia,' Yasmin whispered, not wanting to interrupt.

'Why?' Tia grumbled. 'Just let me do it!'

Yasmin reached out and pulled off the little white label on the beaker.

'It says "H_2O_2", not "H_2O" . . . That's the wrong beaker,' Yasmin kept her voice down; she knew Tia would hate being told what to do in front of the teacher.

'Stop trying to take over the experiment, Yasmin,' Tia snapped.

'I'm not. You're going to make a mistake.'

'Leave her to it, Yassy . . .' Levi said, tugging on Yasmin's trouser leg, but she shook him off.

Tia lifted the spoonful of yeast above the beaker.

Now Yasmin was really agitated.

'That's hydrogen peroxide - H_2O_2! You're going to make a mess!' she yelled, making Miss Zainab whirl round.

'Hydrogen peroxide!?' Miss Zainab's eyes were wide.

'It's *water*, Yasmin. Watch!' Tia smiled smugly and tipped the whole spoonful of yeast into the beaker and shook it.

Instantly the beaker began to foam and bubble, expanding rapidly and bursting out of the top of the container!

Yasmin grabbed the beaker, thankful for the gloves she was wearing, and put it in the deep sink in the corner of the room. The foam continued to pour out of the beaker in a big bubbly mess and Levi suddenly started whooping and clapping.

'Oh, wow. That is *definitely* my favourite experiment! Hehe!' He wiped away tears of laughter before he

saw Yasmin looking at him with a face like thunder.

Miss Zainab rushed over to the sink, ordering Yasmin and Tia to remove their gloves in the sink on the other side of the classroom and wash their hands.

'Hydrogen peroxide! How did this happen? I was so careful with the labelling.'

Tia seemed in shock, but her face had turned

beetroot red and she wouldn't look Yasmin in the eyes. Remi was frantically looking over the calculations in his notebook, trying to make sense of the incident.

Miss Zainab turned to Yasmin in shock. 'Wait, Yasmin. You knew it wasn't water. You knew what the reaction would be!'

Yasmin's throat dried up. Did Miss Zainab think she was responsible for the mix-up?

'Well, I, uh, saw the label. It said "H2O2" . . . The yeast is a catalyst for the decomposition of the hydrogen peroxide . . . I read ahead in the textbook for this term and saw it.'

Miss Zainab stared at her for a moment more before breaking into a huge smile. 'That's correct, Yasmin! Well done! Tia, why didn't you listen to Yasmin? She was trying to warn you.'

Tia opened and closed her mouth, struggling to find any words, before shooting a death glare at Yasmin.

'And, Remi, I thought chemistry was your speciality?' Miss Zainab said.

'It is!' Remi protested. 'Usually . . .'

'You're a team. You need to listen to each other,' Miss Zainab instructed them all. 'Now, I'll clean this up, but we'll have to run the experiment again. You're supposed to be doing this live against Oakmead School this Friday!'

The next thirty minutes were spent in near silence, with Yasmin this time leading the experiment, all the while getting menacing stares from Tia and jealous looks from Remi. By the time the experiment was successfully completed and Miss Zainab was satisfied they knew what they were doing, Yasmin was more than ready to leave.

Yasmin, Tia and Remi packed up their bags in silence and left the lab. Yasmin noticed Levi slip into her rucksack sheepishly and she jostled him about in there for good measure.

Once they were out in the corridor, Tia suddenly turned on her heel and stood directly in front of Yasmin.

'You set us up!' she spat, gesturing to herself and Remi. 'You're trying to make us look bad by sabotaging the experiment.'

Remi looked just as shocked at the accusation as Yasmin, but Tia had firmly placed him by her side.

'I-I didn't. I-I swear . . .' Yasmin stuttered, struggling to find the right words.

'How else did you know the labels were messed up? And you knew it would make a mess! You did that on purpose.' Tia's eyes were blazing and she had crossed her arms defiantly in front of her.

'Yeah . . . that is quite suspicious, Yasmin,' Remi agreed, though he was looking down at the floor and wouldn't meet Yasmin's eyes.

'But . . . but I . . .' Suddenly Yasmin couldn't speak. It felt like how it had before, when her parents had accused her of things that weren't her fault and all she could do was stand there and take it. Why was it so hard to explain things sometimes?

Levi wriggled around in her rucksack wildly, trying to open the zip. 'Let me out! I can fix it! You've gotta tell them you're innocent!'

But Yasmin was frozen to the spot. And when Tia realised she wasn't going to say anything, she smiled triumphantly and strode off, Remi following in her footsteps and muttering something about chemical equations under his breath.

Yasmin watched as they disappeared round the corner and then let go of the breath she hadn't realised she was holding.

'Well done, Levi. I hope you're happy,' she murmured and set off home.

'Explain yourself!'

Yasmin unzipped her bag and shook Levi out on

to her bed. He came tumbling out along with a few school books, some pennies and a chewing-gum wrapper.

'Oof. Watch out, Yasmin. I almost snapped me mobile in half.' Levi held up the small flip phone called the llama landline. Yasmin had discovered it hidden in her book bag when Levi was using it to secretly contact Seen Not Herd. Now he was using it to play a game of Snake.

Yasmin snatched the mobile out of Levi's hands and held it above his head, making him jump up and down on the bed trying to reach it.

'Tell me what you did and you'll get your phone back.' She dangled it just above Levi's nose until he gave up and flopped down on the bed.

'Oh, all right . . . I tampered with the labels. I was only trying to get the teacher to think you was rubbish at science. I thought if you messed up the experiment she'd kick you off the team! Then you could ask your parents to do art club and there'd be nothing in the way for them to say no.' Levi looked up at Yasmin with his best impression of puppy-dog eyes. But with his little beady black eyes it looked like he was trying to summon X-ray vision.

Yasmin tried her best to keep up her stern expression, but eventually she couldn't help but snigger. He looked so silly!

She sat down next to him and he jumped up on to her lap. 'That was a really stupid plan.' Yasmin patted him on the head a bit roughly to show she hadn't fully forgiven him. 'You can't start pulling your old tricks again without telling me. You'll just get us both into trouble!'

Levi sighed. 'I know . . . I just want to get this mission right so badly. It's important, ya know?'

Yasmin's tummy knotted at the thought of what was at stake. A life without Levi.

'I know. But from now on you *have* to share your plans with me. You didn't make me seem rubbish; Miss Zainab thinks I'm some sort of science superhero now.' Yasmin flopped back on the bed in frustration and rubbed her temples.

Levi trotted up the bed to reach her eye level and

peered over. 'Yeah, I did kinda make it worse, didn't I? But I do think you should have a word with her. Find a way to tell her what you really want . . . that you gotta do art club or you'll explode!'

Yasmin chucked a small pillow at Levi. 'It's not Miss Zainab we have to convince. It's Ammi and Papa.'

'Then why don't you just . . . ask them?'

'It isn't that simple. You have to give Ammi and Papa a *reason* why it's better than science. And nothing is better than science to Papa.' Yasmin sighed; it was hard to get Levi to understand her sometimes. If only she could get Ezra to help her handle this pesky llama. If he still wanted to be her friend, that is, after all the lying . . .

'What's up? You look down,' Levi asked, cocking his head to one side.

Yasmin sat up straight, rolled back her shoulders and looked Levi right in his goofy face. 'I hate lying to Ezra. He seems really upset with me.'

'Yeah . . . I did notice.' Levi lay down on the bed and scratched his head. 'That's why I'm gonna suggest something wild.'

Yasmin held her breath and waited for Levi to speak.

'I think . . . I think we should tell him about me.'

Yasmin picked Levi up and hugged him tight.

'Thank you, thank you! But are you sure? If Travis or Mama Llama find out, they'd probably send you back to Peru on the spot.'

'Then we just make sure she don't find out.' Levi shrugged. 'I spent too long helping you make a friend for you to lose him because of me!'

Yasmin set Levi down and looked at him seriously. 'From now on we're in this mission together. You share any plans you have with me, so I can help you make them better. We'll both be Seen Not Herd operatives. Deal?' Yasmin held out her hand.

'We're co-operatives. Co-ops!' Levi stretched out his furry foot and shook Yasmin's hand.

'Deal.'

CHAPTER EIGHT
The ~~Cat~~ Llama's Out of the Bag

Brrrrrrrrrrrrrrrrrrrrrrrrrrrrrrrriiiiiiinnnnnggggg!

As soon as the school bell rang at the end of the following day, Yasmin was legging it across the playground towards the bike sheds, with Levi struggling to keep up behind her.

'Oi, Yasmin! Slow down! Me legs are about two feet shorter than yours.'

Yasmin turned round and impatiently tapped her foot. There were still lots of students milling around, so Levi had to keep freezing or ducking behind lockers to avoid being seen.

'Hurry up, Levi. We're going to miss him. Just let me carry you.'

Levi rolled his eyes but allowed Yasmin to pick him up and rush round the school building to where the bike sheds are. They were rickety old sheets of metal perched on wooden stilts that the students locked their bikes under. The caretaker was often seen hammering yet more nails into the wonky structures to keep them in place.

'Where are we meeting Ezra?' Levi asked. 'I hope it's a secure location.'

'Ummmmm, kind of.' Yasmin reached the end of the school building's grey-stone wall and peered round. When she was certain the coast was clear she pointed and Levi looked .

'The bike shed?' Levi scoffed. 'Well, it's not soundproof or fireproof, but I suppose it'll do.'

'Why would it need to be fireproof?' Yasmin asked. 'Actually don't answer that.'

Under the thin roof of the bike shed was Ezra, looking confused and checking his watch.

'How do you even know that Ezra will believe

you?' Levi craned his neck round the corner, observing Ezra who was standing a little distance away scratching his head.

Yasmin sighed. 'I just have to hope he does.'

Summoning her courage, she strode round the corner and waved at Ezra.

'Hi, Yasmin.' Usually Ezra would have given her a high-five, but he was still a bit angry with her. He wasn't smiling and he had his arms folded. 'I've got to go to my session with Mr J in fifteen minutes. What's going on?'

Yasmin silently pulled out a piece of paper from her pocket and unfolded it. Ezra was one of the few people who understood her even when she didn't speak. And speaking wasn't doing her much good recently. So she'd decided to tell him in the way she knew best, through her comics.

A few months ago, a girl discovered a magical toy Llama in her room.

He was a nightmare and caused trouble wherever he went.

The girl tried everything she could to get rid of him,

but he kept coming back.

One day, the Llama revealed he was actually her guardian.

He had come to teach her to stand up for herself.

And it worked. The girl started speaking again and told her

parents how they needed to listen to her more.

But the Llama's bad behaviour already had him in trouble.

He was turned back into a real Llama and trapped at the farm.

The Llama has been given one last chance to prove he can help the girl.

If he succeeds he'll stay as a toy llama forever.

Ezra looked up from the paper, smiling, and handed it back to Yasmin.

'This is good, Yasmin. But . . . why did you have to show me your new comic in secret?' Ezra leaned back against the bike racks and kicked his feet out in front of him. He'd got even taller over the summer and now his head was almost the height of the bike-shed roof.

'Well . . . because . . . it's real,' Yasmin blurted out.

'Real as in . . . really good?'

Yasmin stood in silence for a while as she watched a look of understanding settle on Ezra's face. He knew she was being serious.

'This happened to you?' he squeaked.

Yasmin nodded.

'But how can a toy be magic?' Ezra asked in a quiet voice.

Yasmin shrugged. Levi had told her about the llama god Urcuchillay and how it chose thirty llamas on a full moon to be turned into toy llamas to serve as agents and guardians of children all over the world. But one thing at a time. Ezra was still coming to terms with one magical toy llama.

'And why is it a llama? That seems random.' Ezra shook his head in disbelief.

'Yeah, it is,' Yasmin agreed.

'Is it . . . is it here right now?' Ezra started looking around him, his eyes darting back and forth.

Yasmin nodded and waited for Levi to show himself. Hopefully he'd be careful about it – there were still a few children about and Ezra looked seriously on edge.

There was a bumping on the roof above them and then a whooshing sound as Levi propelled himself full force off the top, somersaulted in the air and landed in front of Ezra.

'Ta-daaaaaaaaaaaa!' he yelled at the top of his lungs.

'Argh!' Ezra screamed and involuntarily grabbed a broken hockey stick from the ground next to him.

'Whoa, whoa, whoa.' Levi backed up a few paces. 'First you with the tennis racket, Yasmin, and now him with the hockey stick!'

Yasmin stood between them and tried to calm Ezra down.

'It's okay . . . don't worry. This is Levi.' Yasmin slowly stepped away and let Ezra look at him.

'He's alive.' Ezra's eyes looked like they might pop out of his head. 'This . . . is . . . so . . . COOL!'

Ezra reached forward and picked Levi up, letting him sit in his hands.

'Easy does it, mate,' Levi grumbled. 'But at least he thinks I'm cool.'

'You can't hear him, right?' Yasmin asked Ezra, keeping her eye out for anyone nearby.

'No. Wait, is he talking? What's he saying?' Ezra was beaming now, fully immersed in the magic of a talking toy llama. It was pretty unbelievable.

'Smelly bum-fart-breath poo-face,' Levi said directly at Ezra's smiling face.

Yasmin smacked Levi lightly. 'He says nice to meet you.'

'Nice to meet you too, Levi.' Ezra held out a finger and Levi shook it.

Yasmin took a deep breath. 'There's a few more things you need to know . . .'

She briefly filled Ezra in on Seen Not Herd, Mama Llama and the new mission plan. She didn't want to overload him with information but it was important

Ezra knew how serious the secret was. No one else could find out.

'So that's why you've been weird and secretive? There's no Aunt Gail?' Ezra cocked an eyebrow.

'No. There's no Aunt Gail. I'm so sorry for lying, Ezra; I just didn't know what else to do.' Yasmin watched Ezra thinking this over.

Finally, he smiled and said, 'Well . . . I do understand.'

Yasmin was so relieved she gave Ezra a big hug.

Ezra turned to Levi and said, 'So the mission is to help Yasmin get into art club?'

Levi and Yasmin nodded their heads.

'Then I'm in too,' Ezra said proudly. 'Thanks for sharing your secret with me, Yasmin. This is the best thing that's happened . . . ever!'

Yasmin smiled at her friend. 'I guess it is quite cool now that I have someone to share it with. But Mama Llama, Seen Not Herd and everyone else can't find out about this. It has to be top secret.'

'Understood.' Ezra saluted to emphasise the point.

PLOP!

All three of them looked up to see a pigeon flying away.

'Oh, gross, did it poo?' Ezra checked over his arms and patted his head.

But Levi had hopped on to the seat of a bike and was looking at the ground. With surprising agility he climbed down the frame of the bike and picked up the small object that had plopped next to them. It was a tiny note.

'What does it say?' Yasmin asked.

Levi cleared his voice and read the note aloud, with Yasmin relaying the message to Ezra.

Agent Levi, Operative no. 432

The Mama Llama has landed. Expect her arrival shortly. She will be supervising the progress of your mission. Do not fail.

This message will self-destruct in ten seconds.

Yasmin was dubious. 'Self-destruct? How?'

But Levi tossed the message away from them. 'Run!' he yelled, causing Yasmin and Ezra to scramble behind the brick wall. They covered their ears and braced for impact, watching as the note went *poof* in a small cloud of smoke.

Levi got up from the ground and dusted himself off. 'Well . . . that was anticlimactic.'

CHAPTER NINE
Scientific Sabotage!

BUMP...

BUMP...

BUMP...

If you've ever travelled in the back of a rickety school minibus that looks like it was made in the Jurassic era, you'll be familiar with this sound.

BUMP...

BUMP...

BUMP...

You'll also be familiar with the lurching feeling your stomach makes every time the minibus hits a dip or a speed bump and you're propelled five feet into the air, clutching on to your seat belt for dear life.

This is the fate Yasmin faced as she, Levi and the Funsen Burner team made their way to Oakmead

School that Friday afternoon for the first heat of the London Optimal Science Education tournament, also known as LOSE.

(The organisers didn't notice the unfortunate acronym until they'd already got the posters printed.)

Since Tia was still convinced that Yasmin had tried to sabotage their experiment in practice earlier that week, and Remi was too frightened to oppose Tia, Yasmin had been pushed to the back of the bus, while her team mates sat upfront with Miss Zainab, who was driving. Yasmin didn't mind. She'd planned to use the journey for napping since her brothers had arrived home from Pakistan at 3am the night before. They'd, of course, come running into her room and jumped on the bed to make sure she knew they were home. But the bumpy bus was definitely not a napping environment.

'Oooof, this bus ride is giving me a dicky tummy.' Levi was on Yasmin's lap, clinging on to her seat belt. 'I'm gonna vom.'

Yasmin was quite sure that toy llamas couldn't be sick, but she picked up a tissue and placed it under his head just in case.

'Thanks, love.' Levi hung his head limply to one side. 'Now, don't forget the plan – you've gotta throw the competition.'

'I'm not doing that,' Yasmin whispered back, bracing herself as the van skidded round a corner.

'Why not?' Levi held on to his stomach. 'If you look like you're rubbish at science, they'll kick you off the te-aaaaaaaaaaaaam.' The minibus had come screeching to a halt.

Yasmin sighed, looking out of the window. They'd reached Oakmead School. 'I always have to try my best. And I'd embarrass my parents if I got kicked off. I can't do that.'

'Argh, you're too good, Yassy.' Levi clambered off her lap and looked out of the window too. 'Wooo, this place is fancy.'

Oakmead School was a large red-brick building with multiple decorated entrances and those stone statues that look like creepy faces coming out of the walls. There was a spacious outside paved area where a small team of smiling faces waved at the minibus. The competition.

'Come on, everyone. We don't want to keep our hosts waiting!' Miss Zainab shouted from the driver's seat. 'Goggles and lab coats on, Funsen Burners. Let's make a good impression.'

Yasmin didn't think that three bedraggled children with mild nausea in lab coats was a great impression, but oh well.

The three kids slid out of the minibus and Miss Zainab slammed the door shut behind them. Yasmin

had sewn a special pocket into the inside of her lab coat so that Levi could come with her. They were working together now and she'd learned from experience that bad things tended to happen when the llama was left up to his own devices.

'Welcome, Fish Lane Primary!' the rival team chorused in perfect unison. Their lab coats were personalised with their names stitched on to each in swirling script.

Lucien
Avery
Edward

Taking a quick glance at her team mates' faces, Yasmin could tell that Remi was terrified of the competition, Tia hated them all and Miss Zainab was just happy to be there.

The teacher from Oakmead stepped forward with a straight face. 'I'm Mr Johnson. We're so pleased you're joining us for an afternoon of scientific discovery. Please follow me into the hall.'

Mr Johnson was almost as wide and tall as the school, and Yasmin noticed many of the other students around gave him a wide berth as they walked through the lofty corridors.

'Yassy, I think now would be a great time to tell Miss Zainab how you really feel,' Levi suggested. 'I've even prepared a list of science-based jokes you can use to break the ice.'

'I don't think that's a good idea,' Yasmin hissed.

'Course it is! Listen: how does the moon cut his hair . . .? E-clipse it!' Levi laughed. 'Get it? Like he clips it . . . but it's "eclipse" . . .'

Yasmin bit her lip and was extremely grateful that she was the only one who could hear him.

She was surprised to see that that the 'school hall' was more like a concert hall! There was a stage on which two tables had been set up for LOSE with a podium in-between. All around the sides of the stage were big red curtains that hid the wings and backstage area. The ceiling was so high that there was even a balcony that ran round the sides of the hall.

The two teams took their seats at the tables with Mr Johnson taking his place at the podium. Yasmin looked at the big clock at the back of the school hall and wished it would speed up. All she wanted to do was go home and work on *LOUDMOUTH*. The deadline for the competition was approaching and she still had so much shading to do ... not to mention the final chapters! But instead she was here, sitting at a table with two team mates who hated her and a stuffed llama in her pocket.

Wait ...

Yasmin patted the secret pocket where Levi was supposed to be. *He'd gone!*

CHAPTER TEN
Buzzers at the Ready!

'Okay, question one,' Mr Johnson announced to the small audience of teachers and students from the school, 'is a chemistry question. What is the first element on the periodic table?'

There was no time to look for Levi; the quiz had already started. Yasmin panicked, what was the question again?

BzZ.

Oakmead buzzed in first and Lucien, smiling, leaned towards his microphone. 'Hydrogen.'

Mr Johnson smiled. 'That is correct, Lucien. Well done.'

Suddenly Yasmin spotted Levi underneath her table. He was holding some sort of tool . . .

'Second question. What orbits the nucleus of an

atom?' Mr Johnson puffed his chest out and looked expectantly at his team.

Tia tried to buzz but Oakmead beat her to it – again.

'Electrons,' Edward said assuredly, then smiled at Tia.

Yasmin was starting to think those smiles were more menacing then friendly . . .

She tried to kick Levi but he was still under the table fiddling about with something. Yasmin slid down in her chair a little to see what he was doing. He had a pair of wire cutters and was messing about with the wires that went into their buzzers! He was trying to sabotage their chances!

'Yasmin!' Tia whispered aggressively. 'Are you even listening? You missed question three!'

'Sorry,' Yasmin mumbled. At the next question she made sure she pressed the buzzer as quickly as possible but it still didn't go off. Levi . . . She was going to lock him up in the minibus the second she got the chance.

After a few more rounds with their buzzer not going off and Oakmead getting all the points, Mr Johnson called a short break for the teams to get some water.

As soon as everyone else had dispersed from the stage, Levi jumped up on to the table and hopped on to the buzzer.

BzZ!

'Ta-da!' he announced to Yasmin, doing a little tap dance.

But Yasmin whacked him around the head. 'What happened to working together?' she hissed, careful not to let anyone see her. 'You cut our wires.'

Levi scratched his head. 'Uhhh, no. I fixed your wires. See?' He pressed the buzzer again and a sharp **BzZ**, went off. Okay, now Yasmin was confused.

'I noticed your buzzers weren't going off so I hopped underneath to take a look and guess what? They weren't even connected! I think that Mr Johnson isn't playing by the rules. I'm not having your voice be ignored again!' Levi shook his head and tutted.

'Do you think Oakmead are cheating?' A knot of anger formed in Yasmin's stomach but she shook it away. 'No...I need to concentrate on the competition. Even though I know where I'd rather be.'

Yasmin stood up and stretched, trying to focus her mind. Tia and Remi had been trying to buzz in and answer every question in the last round whilst she was worrying about Levi. She was going to have to work twice as hard in the next round to make up for those lost points.

'Don't worry, love. We'll get you into art club,' Levi said as Yasmin prepared their table for the experiment. 'I'll find a way . . . I've got to.'

Then Mr Johnson announced the next round – the live experiment.

Yasmin smiled sadly and patted Levi on the head before filling a beaker with water.

But out of the corner of his beady little eye, Levi

saw something. Something that Yasmin didn't notice.

As the next round began Yasmin, Tia and Remi waited patiently for their turn to perform the yeast-blowing-up-a-balloon experiment. Oakmead went first and Mr Johnson was hovering over them like an angry wasp, flitting about but unable to give them any pointers. Avery was in charge this time and he didn't seem happy about it. His cheeks were flushed red and his hands were sweating so much that the beaker slipped from his palms. Yasmin noticed he only put in half the amount of yeast required of the experiment as he fumbled the measurements. Mr Johnson groaned and muttered something to Avery which made him even more flustered. Yasmin felt sorry for the boy, even if he was her competition. Mr Johnson was taking this far too seriously.

Somehow, the balloons over Avery's table started to inflate. A little at first and then bigger and bigger.

Mr Johnson clapped his hands together, 'Well done Avery, a brilliant example of the experiment in action.'

But Yasmin knew there wasn't enough yeast in his beaker to give off that much gas. Something fishy was going on.

A high-pitched whistle made Yasmin look up and there was Levi! He'd somehow run a thin wire across the hall between the balcony that ran either side.

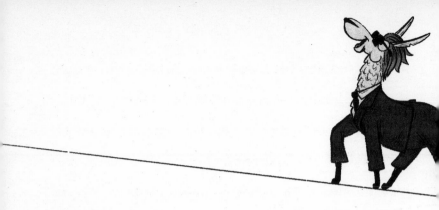

Now he was edging across it, hanging perilously over the stage.

'Even though I still think this competition is stupid,' Levi yelled, as he hung over the left-hand side of the stage on the wire. 'I'm not gonna let you lose because the other team is cheating!'

Levi jumped off the wire, flew through the air and clung on to the red curtains that

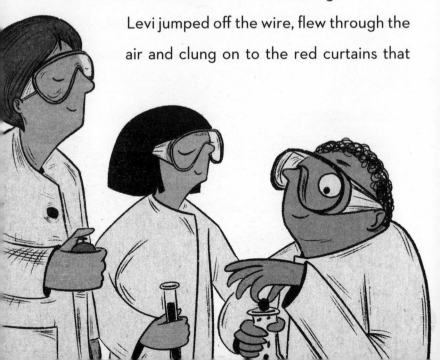

hung around the wings

of the stage. Yasmin watched in horror as the whole

of the curtain hanging over the left-hand side of the

stage came crashing down to the floor.

The whole room gasped at the sudden commotion.

The curtains falling down had revealed the wings

where a small boy in an Oakmead uniform was

sitting next to an air pump. He took one look at the stunned audience and then another at Mr Johnson before legging it backstage where he could hide.

'What exactly is going on here?' Miss Zainab strode on to the stage her hands on her hips.

Mr Johnson tried to block her path, 'I'm not too sure but it seems like a harmless prank.'

But Miss Zainab couldn't be fooled. She pointed to the air pump and traced a line with her finger all the way to the table where Avery was doing his experiment. 'There's a see-through pipe running from the air pump to your pupil's table, blowing up his balloons. I couldn't see it from down in the audience but now I'm up-close it's very clear. Your team has been cheating."

Mr Johnson looked repeatedly between Miss Zainab and his team, unsure of where to settle his gaze. The audience waited with bated breath. This revelation was much more exciting than the school science competition they had expected to see.

Finally, Mr Johnson looked at Avery.

'Avery, I can't believe you would cheat! I, of course, had nothing to do with this matter and I highly condemn cheating in any manner.'

'But Sir I–'

'Go to my office immediately and wait for me there.' Mr Johnson ordered, unwilling to hear Avery's defence.

'This competition is over. We'll have to do a rematch at a later date.' Miss Zainab announced, her voice echoing around the hall. 'Children, go back to the minibus. We are finished here.'

The image of Levi hanging from the wire stayed with Yasmin as they BUMP-BUMP-BUMPed all the way home in the minibus. She'd managed to pick Levi out of the folds of the curtains heaped on the floor as they left – not without Tia noticing and raising an eyebrow.

Now Yasmin held him tightly in her hands to stop him from hitting the roof of the minibus on the next speedbump.

'Thanks for helping us out back there.' Yasmin whispered to him. 'But why do you look so sad? Or are you actually going to vomit!?'

Levi looked out the window. 'No, no it's not that . . . I saw Mama Llama.'

Yasmin's mouth flew open. Mama Llama had been at Oakmead?

'She looked so unimpressed.' Levi's head drooped into Yasmin's palms.

'But you helped reveal the other team were cheating! Without you we would have lost.' Yasmin's voice rose in volume at the injustice, before she remembered she had company in the minibus.

'I know but my mission isn't to help you in the science team! In fact, I've probably made things a lot worse by keeping you in the competition . . . I just couldn't stand the other team cheating!' Levi stopped ranting and took a deep breath.

'So you ruined your chances of passing the mission just to help me?' Yasmin gently rubbed Levi's small furry head with a finger. 'If Mama Llama can't see that's what a good guardian llama does then she's bonkers. Don't worry Levi, we'll find a way to get me into art club.'

'Yeah . . . we'll find a way.' Levi agreed, but his glass eyes still looked distinctly worried. Yasmin felt uneasy. Mama Llama had seen Levi do the exact opposite of what his mission was meant to be – he'd kept her *in* the science team. Would this mean he'd be sent back to Peru? How could she stand school, science team and her parents without him?

'Hey, Yasmin!'

Tia had turned round from her seat at the front and was waving at Yasmin to get her attention.

'At least you sabotaged the other team this time.'

'But I didn't sabotage anything!' Yasmin protested.

'I saw that weird llama toy you carry around left in

the curtains. You obviously rigged them to fall down.' Tia had clearly convinced Remi of this too as he was nodding along.

'Couldn't you have waited until *after* I did the experiment though?' Remi pouted, 'I never got to have a go . . .'

'But I really didn't–'

Tia pouted, holding up a hand. 'Save it. I don't care. I just wanted to tell you that my mum is making me invite you to my party. It's laser tag. She said to invite the whole class so . . .'

Yasmin searched for the right words but by the time she was ready to say something Tia and Remi had turned back round.

Laser tag with her arch-nemesis. Great.

CHAPTER ELEVEN
Laser Chaser Showdown

'Pew-pew-pew!' Ezra was firing pretend lasers at Levi who was dodging and diving. They were walking along an empty street to Laser Chaser: 'East London's premier laser tag and Chinese takeaway venue'. It was the only place you could get a spring roll while shooting electric light beams at your mates.

Of course Yasmin had tried to get out of going. Tia didn't want her there and Yasmin didn't want to be there either. But Tia's mum had already rung Ammi to tell her the party details so it was set in stone. To Yasmin's parents refusing a party invite was the ultimate insult. When Cousin Meena had her wedding party and Cousin Aktar's wife had refused to go, it was all anyone spoke about for a month after. It turned out Cousin Aktar's wife had broken her leg, but everyone still thought she was extremely rude for not going. So Yasmin was attending Tia's birthday party.

'ENDOFSTORY,' as Ammi had said.

At least she had Ezra and Levi for support.

'Pew-PEW! I definitely got you that time, Levi,' Ezra said, chuckling.

'As if!' Levi stuck his tongue out and ran on ahead.

Ezra grinned. 'It's so fun having a magical llama, Yasmin. It's like having a dog.'

'What did he just call me?' Levi was outraged.

Yasmin laughed. 'That's because you can't hear him, Ezra.' Yasmin rolled her eyes. 'Then you might find it less fun.'

Suddenly Levi skidded to a stop and held a finger to his mouth. Ezra and Yasmin took his cue and froze.

'What is it?' Yasmin whispered out of the corner of her mouth.

Levi jumped up into Yasmin's arms and motioned behind him with a leg. 'We've got company. Don't look now.'

Ignoring his advice, Yasmin whirled round and caught sight of a small fluffy thing before it slipped into an alley. It was quick, but she was certain she saw a flash of sandy hair and red spectacles.

'Mama Llama,' Yasmin breathed. 'Is she going to follow you everywhere now?'

'It's part of her monitoring my progress on the mission,' Levi grumbled. 'She's even giving me directions now through this earpiece. I only wanted it to complete the outfit but now she's hooked it up to her phone so she can talk to me at all times!'

Ezra looked back from Yasmin to Levi, unable to hear one half of the conversation. 'Fill me in. I want to help!'

Yasmin kept her voice low and beckoned Ezra over. 'Mama Llama is tracking us. You have to play it cool and pretend you don't know about Levi.

Otherwise we'll all be in trouble.'

'Roger that.' Ezra straightened his back and walked on ahead, whistling and trying to act 'casual'.

As the three of them reached the laser tag venue, Levi jumped up into Yasmin's pocket. She'd worn her denim dungarees especially so he'd have somewhere to sit where he could still see out. Tia already thought she was weird, so Yasmin figured that carrying around a stinky toy llama like a kangaroo baby wouldn't make it much worse.

Yasmin groaned as they reached the Laser Chaser entrance, where a few of their schoolmates had already gathered.

'I'm going to the party of someone who basically told me they didn't want me to come. Am I the biggest loser in the world?' Yasmin looked at Ezra and Levi in turn.

'Nooooo, of course not.' Ezra put a hand on her shoulder, but his voice wasn't too convincing.

'Look at it this way, love,' Levi piped up. 'Rather than being a loser, why not be a winner? This is ya chance to beat Tia at something.'

Yasmin's eyes lit up. 'Yeah . . . maybe you're right, Levi. And I bet, if I beat Tia at laser tag she'll be so annoyed that she'll ask Miss Zainab to kick me off the team.'

Ezra looked at Yasmin out of the corner of her eye. 'That seems a bit drastic, Yasmin. You could just . . . ask Miss Zainab to leave?'

But Yasmin's head was already whirring with ideas. Yes, she'd beat Tia and Remi so that they'd hate her *even more* and tell Miss Zainab there was *no way* they could work with her. She'd be kicked off the team without having to throw the competition and then her parents would have to let her choose another activity!

'It's the perfect plan!' she announced, her fists curled in determination.

'Is it?' Ezra questioned.

Yasmin narrowed her eyes as she saw her arch-nemesis Tia standing with her mum. 'I'm going to beat Tia at laser tag . . .'

They headed inside and said a brief hello to Tia and her mum. Her mum looked like Tia, except taller, thinner and with white-blonde hair in perfect curls. Yasmin noticed that almost everything Tia's mum wore had a brand name on it – most of them she'd never heard of before.

'For goodness' sake, Tia. I told you not to wear the orange dress; it doesn't suit you at all,' Tia's mum muttered as she pulled at her daughter's clothes, fussing over the placement of her neckline.

'Mum, get off,' Tia muttered back, her eyes darting around to see whether anyone had noticed.

Yasmin quickly looked away. She was glad that her parents at least let her wear whatever she wanted. Unless it was a 'family gathering' in which case she always had to wear the vibrant monstrosities her aunties picked out for her: a lime-green shalwar kameez, a rhinestone dupatta. Yasmin had worn some of fashion's worst creations to keep her aunties happy.

She put clothes out of her mind – she had to stay focused. Yasmin was determined to play the best laser tag match of her life that day, and with Levi as a second pair of eyes and ears she liked her chances.

All was eerily quiet in the laser tag arena . . . too quiet.

It was every man (and woman and llama) for themselves as Tia had decided she didn't want to do teams. There would be only one winner. So, as soon as the siren had gone off, every single player had run off in opposite directions to find shelter.

It was a cavernous room with screens and walls set up to make it look like a maze. Yasmin was glad she'd gone for her denim dungarees as the whole arena was lit only by a black light, which made the UV-painted walls and any white clothing shine like a beacon.

Ezra had run off yelling, 'CHARGE!' almost immediately, so Yasmin knew she couldn't count on him to have her back when it came to laser tag. She crept silently round the side of a screen, holding her laser gun tightly to her chest. For a game that didn't involve any real danger her heart was beating very loudly. Luckily she'd placed Levi in her back pocket so that she'd be covered from all angles, and it was paying off.

'Yasmin, behind you!' Levi called.

Yasmin whipped round and aimed. She fired a single shot.

Zoop!

And hit Remi right in the tummy.

'Arghh! You scared me, Yasmin,' Remi said, then frowned. 'I didn't want to play this anyway; the lasers aren't even scientific standard.' He trudged back to the entrance, giving Yasmin a sour look as he went.

Yasmin and Levi high-fived. 'Well done, guardian llama,' Yasmin whispered, before dropping to a crouch and pacing forward once more.

Her gaze was steady; her grip was firm. She felt like a special forces commando in the middle of the jungle, when she was actually in a warehouse in Whitechapel.

'White T-shirt, six o'clock!' Levi yelled.

Yasmin dropped to her knees and rolled behind a crate, firing off two quick zoop-zoops as she went.

'Ugh, nooooo.' It was Betty, a girl from her class, who had got hit. 'Who even was that?'

Yasmin backed up into the shadows and out of sight.

'Look at you – you're like a ninja.' Levi's eyes were wide. 'I'm well proud . . . and also a bit scared.'

'Oh . . .' Yasmin grinned. 'It's only just begun. Time to find Tia.'

CHAPTER TWELVE
The Birthday Ruiner

'Levi, what happened?' Yasmin dropped to her knees and cradled Levi's head in her hands.

He gave a few coughs and spluttered. 'It was Tia. She snuck up in my blind spot and got me. Mama Llama's been going on at me in the earpiece; it distracted me.' He stuck his tongue out of one side of his mouth and dramatically hung his body limply. 'Avenge me, Yasmin . . . Avenge . . . me . . .'

'I will. Don't worry. I'm going to find Tia and beat her!' Yasmin jumped to her feet and scanned her surroundings.

'All right, good.' Levi quickly stopped his 'dying' routine and trotted off in the direction of the exit. 'I'd better find Mama Llama and see what she wants.'

BING-BONG.

The sound played over the speakers of the laser arena.

'There are now just two players left in the game. I repeat, there are two players left in the game. You are now playing for the title of champion.'

Yasmin's stomach lurched with nerves, but she was determined. She'd made it this far on adrenaline and focus. But that was because she had Levi by her (back) side. He gave her all the confidence she needed, but now he wasn't here . . . she just felt small again.

Is this what life would always feel like if he got sent back to Peru?

There was the sound of running footsteps to her left behind a low wall and Yasmin jumped for cover. Tia. She'd hit Levi with her laser, probably aiming for Yasmin. A new feeling welled up in Yasmin's chest and she knew it would see her through to the end of the showdown. Revenge.

Yasmin crawled along by the screen where she'd

heard Tia's footsteps. An idea sprang into her mind. She took off one shoe and edged her way along the UV-painted wall, towards a gap between all the screens. She held her laser gun tightly and hopped up to a crouch, perched on the balls of her feet, breathing steadily.

'This is for Levi.'

She launched her shoe at the clearing, letting it knock against the wall. Sure enough came the sound of running feet and a PEW brought Tia racing out from her cover.

'Ha! Got you, Yasmin . . . Huh?' Tia looked wildly round to where she'd expected to find Yasmin.

'Too bad, Tia.' Yasmin aimed her laser gun. 'You lose!'

With a final PEW Yasmin shot a single laser at Tia's chest, hitting her as she jumped to the ground for cover.

The siren wailed again to signal the end of the game and the lights in the arena came up. Yasmin stood stock-still staring at Tia. She'd beat her . . . so why did she feel so rubbish?

'Ugh, you're so *annoying*, Yasmin. I bet you cheated!' Tia shouted.

'I didn't cheat – you're just angry that you're a loser!' Yasmin shouted back, the words tumbling out of her mouth. Uh-oh . . .

'It's my birthday – you should have let me win, weirdo!' Tia stuck her tongue out.

'You're the weirdo and you're mean! And you're rubbish at science. I bet Miss Zainab only let you in the team because she felt sorry for you.' Yasmin's face was red hot and her hands were shaking, but she couldn't stop the words that were pouring from her brain and straight out her mouth.

Tia looked like she might explode. Picking herself up, she stomped past Yasmin and towards the exit. It was only then that Yasmin realised that the whole class, Tia's mum, and Levi and Ezra had rushed in to see who the winner was. Instead, they saw both girls having a full-on shouting match.

'Tia, honey, don't cry. It makes your face go all red and puffy,' Tia's mum said in front of everyone, pulling her daughter towards her. But Tia pushed her away and stormed out of the door, but not before turning back to say one last thing.

'Yasmin Shah, you have ruined my birthday.'

Yasmin, Ezra and Levi were sitting on the wall outside Laser Chaser in the darkening light. Ammi was coming to pick them up. Neither had said a word since the party had abruptly ended and Ezra had taken to awkwardly drumming on his lap to fill the silence. Levi was unusually quiet too but Yasmin was too down in the dumps to ask him why.

She was a birthday ruiner. That was probably the worst thing you could be, other than a criminal. She'd let her silly mission of getting out of science club ruin Tia's birthday. Even if she was mean, it wasn't Tia's fault that Yasmin couldn't do the club she wanted. She'd said such horrible things to Tia in front of everyone. Why couldn't she keep those thoughts to herself?

'I should just stop speaking again,' she mumbled finally. 'I only upset people.'

'No, that's not true!' Ezra protested. 'You just got a bit too into laser tag.'

'But I said such nasty things to Tia . . .'

'Nah, love, it's my fault,' Levi chimed in. 'I'm supposed to be helping ya.'

Yasmin cocked an eyebrow. 'With art club, yeah. But this doesn't have anything to do with the mission.'

Levi looked like he was about to say something else, but instead his mouth stayed hanging open and his gaze fixed forward. Yasmin followed his eyeline.

From behind a holly bush Mama Llama emerged, dressed in a trench coat and sunglasses with an earpiece of her own. She nodded her head coolly and motioned to Levi to join her.

This was definitely not good. Levi gulped and jumped down from the wall. As he approached, they both slipped through the gap between the holly bush and the wall of the Laser Chaser building for privacy. Not on Yasmin's watch – she was determined to know what was going on.

She made a gesture to Ezra to follow her and they silently tiptoed towards the gap, ducking behind a dirty old van to keep them covered. Yasmin cupped her ear with one hand. She wasn't sure whether it actually helped you hear better but she'd seen people do it on the TV so thought it was worth a shot.

'I hear what ya sayin' . . .' She heard Levi's voice, even though he was far away. This was the first time she'd been thankful for his loud mouth.

'No, I don't think you do, Agent,' Mama Llama's rich and commanding voice interrupted. 'Clearly your child's communication has not improved if she's having shouting matches with her peers.'

Yasmin shook her head in confusion. 'My communication?'

'What are they saying?' Ezra said, nudging her, but Yasmin shushed him and listened carefully.

'Perhaps if you hadn't spent so long messing about in science practice, you wouldn't have failed your mission. I mean, did you really think any of those methods would work?'

There was a fraught pause.

'Failed?' Levi said in a small voice.

Mama Llama sighed. 'Yes, Agent. You failed. This is the end of the line. I must report back to the London paddock to arrange your return to Peru. I will allow you to go back to your child's house while you await further instructions to ease the transition for her. But you must stay there.'

Yasmin stopped listening and her hand dropped limply to her side. She felt completely numb with shock.

'What is it, Yasmin?' Ezra nudged her. 'What's going on?'

Yasmin turned to him slowly, trying desperately to force the words out.

'L-Levi failed. He's being sent back . . . and it's my fault.'

CHAPTER THIRTEEN
One Last Plan

It was dark by the time Yasmin, Ezra and Levi got home. The walk back had been quiet and seemed longer than usual. Ammi didn't ask many questions, which was highly unusual, so Yasmin guessed the look on their faces must have put her off.

As they walked up the stairs with Yasmin in the lead there was music blaring from the room above and Yasmin groaned. Yep, her brothers were definitely home.

Even after a summer stay with super-strict Daadi, her brothers hadn't toned down their pranks. After all, they had managed to pull off that spider prank across continents.

Yasmin positioned herself in front of Ezra who was carrying Levi and walked up the creaking stairs.

She reached the familiar closed door of her brother's room with the 'No Girls Allowed' sign on the door and sighed. So immature. She flung the door open and walked in but immediately felt something push against her face like an invisible screen.

She cried out, scrabbling at her face before realising it was cling film. Her brothers must have taped it across the door and waited for her to come.

Tall Brother and Short Brother were in hysterics, rolling around on their beds and copying Yasmin's scream.

'Oh my god, you should have seen your face!' Tall Brother guffawed.

'You were like, "Arghhhhh, what is it?!"' Short Brother was literally wiping tears from his eyes.

It wasn't that funny.

She rolled her eyes at them. 'Good to see you've grown up since being away!'

'Whoa, sorry, Trombone!' Short Brother exclaimed, still unused to hearing her voice.

'Yeah, are you in a bad mood because you got annihilated in laser tag?' Tall Brother asked.

Yasmin ignored them and walked past. She really didn't want to be having this conversation right now.

Ezra walked past them too, head held high in solidarity with Yasmin. But before he left the room he turned back and said, 'Actually, Yasmin won,' leaving the brothers open-mouthed in surprise.

When they were in her room she slammed the door behind them, which just about blocked out the sound of her brothers' awful music.

Finally, sitting glumly in a little circle on her bed, Yasmin and Ezra got the whole story from Levi.

'So . . . I spoke with Mama Llama-' Levi began.

'I know. I heard it all,' Yasmin interrupted.

Levi's eyes went wide. 'Wait, you could hear her too?' He scratched his head with a furry leg. 'First Travis, now Mama Llama. You should only be able to hear me cos I'm your guardian llama.'

Yasmin shrugged. 'I guess I can hear all the llamas.

But that's not what I want to know. Why was Mama Llama talking about my "communication"?'

Ezra leaned forward, waiting for Levi's response even though he knew he wouldn't hear it.

If it was possible for toy llamas to blush, then Levi got pretty close. 'Uh, well . . . the truth is my mission wasn't really to get you into art club. It was to help you learn how to communicate.'

'What?' Yasmin was outraged. 'Levi says his real mission was to help me learn to communicate,' she told Ezra.

'What does that mean?' Ezra was just as confused as Yasmin. 'But he already helped you learn how to talk.'

'Talking ain't the same as communicating.' Levi sighed. 'Communicating is, well, it's getting someone to understand the things you're saying.'

'Why didn't you just tell me what the real mission was then? We could have helped!' Yasmin felt herself getting frustrated.

'Cos then it would have been forced,' Levi retorted.

'Maybe it would have felt forced,' Ezra added.

'That's what Levi said.' Yasmin held her fingers to her temples. This was getting confusing. 'You were meant to teach me to communicate but really you were lying the whole time!'

'I'm sorry, Yassy.' Levi got up and put an arm on her hand. 'But it wasn't lying completely. If you could communicate to your parents and teachers why you wanted to do art club, that would have completed the mission too! But you were so against just asking for what you wanted. I thought if I could find a way of getting you out of science club first, it would be easier. I did really want you to be able to communicate with people, though. If I told you that's what the mission was, you'd be doing it for me. Not for yourself.'

Suddenly, all Yasmin's anger fell away and the crushing reality hit her. Levi was leaving.

'B-but we are co-ops . . .' Yasmin started sobbing. It was a big ugly cry that made her nose all snotty.

Ezra gave her a tight squeeze.

'Don't cry, Yassy, or you'll get me going!' Levi wailed before he burst into tears too. 'You two are the b-b-best mates I ever had!' he said between sobs.

They were just one boy, one girl and one magical stuffed llama crying and hugging on a Saturday night.

If it wasn't for Ammi yelling up the stairs, who knows how long the pity party would have gone on for?

'YASMINCOMEDOWNHERE. TIA'SMUMJUSTRANG.'

Yasmin and Ezra looked at each other with wide eyes. Uh-oh.

Yasmin took a deep breath and wiped her face dry with her duvet. 'Stay here. I'm going to fix this,' she said, getting up from bed with a new purpose.

'What are you going to do?' Ezra called after her.

'I'm going to communicate. I'm telling my parents I want to do art club and that's that.'

Ezra and Levi gave each other a look but there was no stopping Yasmin. She'd already stomped out of her room and down the first flight of stairs.

'Ohhhh, you're in trouble,' Short Brother teased as she walked through their room.

'Yeah, Ammi sounds *really angry*,' Tall Brother

goaded, checking out a new cap in the mirror.

Yasmin ignored them and continued stomping down the stairs, through her parents' empty bedroom and into her aunties' room.

Auntie Gigi stepped in front of her, taking Yasmin by the shoulders. 'Yasmin, honey, what did you do?'

'Yes we couldn't help but . . . overhear the phone call . . .' Auntie Bibi sucked air in through her teeth to get across the point about how bad it was.

Yasmin didn't have time for this. They'd obviously picked up the phone in their room to listen in to Ammi's call. Yasmin shook herself free of Auntie Gigi's grip and hurried down the stairs to the kitchen.

Her pace slowed as she realised she was about to face her parents' wrath. But Levi was being sent back to Peru because she couldn't communicate. Even if Levi had failed, she wanted to show him and Mama Llama that she could communicate what she needed. She had to make her parents understand how important art was to her.

'YASMINWHYDIDYOURUINTIA'SBIRTHDAY?'

Ammi was sitting at the head of
the kitchen table and Papa
was hovering beside her.
Both of them were glaring
so angrily that their eyes
might as well have been
lasers too.

'But, Ammi, I–'

'We brought you up
to be a respectful girl.'
Papa shook his head.
'You represent this family
whenever you leave the
house. Don't you know that?'

'Yes, but–'

'NOBUTS!
TIAHASBEENCRYINGALLEVENING.'
Ammi gesticulated so wildly with her hands
that she almost hit Papa in the face.

'What do you have to say for yourself, hmm?' Papa folded his arms and raised his eyebrows.

'I-I . . .' Yasmin looked from Ammi to Papa and back again. 'I WANT TO DO ART CLUB!'

There was a short, confused silence, which actually helped to break the anger a bit. Yasmin ploughed on, letting the words take over. 'I love art and I want to do art club so I can work on my comic but it's at the same time as stupid science team, which I hate, and art makes me feel happy and calm so I want to switch, okay? There, I said it!' Yasmin took a deep breath and looked at the unreadable expressions on her parents' faces.

It suddenly dawned on her that asking for something in the middle of a telling-off *might not* have been the best timing.

'What does art club have to do with anything?' her papa finally bellowed. 'With this behaviour you're lucky we even let you do science team!'

'HOWDAREYOUDEMANDTHINGSLIKETHIS?'

Ammi agreed. 'GOTOYOURROOM!'

Yasmin's face turned bright red as she sprinted out of the kitchen. She knew for sure her aunties, her brothers and probably even Ezra and Levi had heard the entire conversation. She put her hands over her ears and rushed as fast as she could up all the flights of stairs, ignoring her aunties and her brothers and slamming the door to her room.

She jumped on to the bed and buried her face in the covers.

'So . . . it didn't go well?' Ezra ventured, pretending to read one of her books.

'No.'

'Yassy . . . communicating don't mean just telling people what you want,' Levi explained gently. 'It's about understanding each other.'

'Well, how am I supposed to know that? I only started talking a few months ago.' Yasmin rolled over on to her back and gloomily looked at the ceiling. 'I don't want to lose you, Levi.'

'Me neither. I only just met you!' Ezra agreed, picking Levi up and squeezing him tight.

'Whooooa, go easy there,' Levi wheezed. 'You'll be all right; you've got each other.'

Yasmin tried to stop the tears that pricked at her eyes. 'Will you ring us when you're back in Peru, so we can tell you what's going on?'

Levi said nothing and jumped out of Ezra's hands, going to stand at the window. He looked out at the city with a serious expression.

'The thing is, once you lose your licence and you're turned back into a real llama . . . you lose all your memories of being a toy. I won't remember any of this . . . or either of you . . .'

Yasmin felt like a ton of bricks had crashed down on her head. No, no, she couldn't let that happen. There'd been many times when Yasmin had felt forgotten or overlooked by her family in the past. Levi was the first person (okay, *llama*) who saw her for who she really was.

She got up and looked at the big chalkboard behind her bed. This was where she planned out sketches and comics. She'd even planned out Levi's escape from City Farm here before . . . Which gave her an idea.

'We aren't giving up. Not yet,' she announced. 'Are you willing to try one more thing?'

Ezra's face brightened and he stood up. 'Yeah! Count me in!'

Levi turned round slowly and looked at Yasmin through narrowed eyes. 'What do you plan on doing?'

Yasmin hopped up on her bed and picked up a piece of thick chalk. 'Well, let's think. So, here's you, Levi.' Yasmin drew a quick sketch of Levi on the chalkboard. She drew a circle round him and some lines coming out of him.

'You became a magical toy llama when Urcuchillay, the god of the llamas, chose you to become a guardian llama.' She drew her best impression of a llama god at the end of one of the lines.

'The llama god! Coooool.' Ezra's eyes were wide.

'But in order to stay here as a toy llama you had to keep your llama licence.' Yasmin drew a little licence at the end of one of the lines.

'But we know how that went,' Levi added.

Yasmin nodded and drew a cross through the picture of the licence. She chewed her lip and thought hard. 'Well, there must be a way to get past all this mission stuff and keep you as a toy llama. We're missing the bigger picture here . . .'

All three of them stared at the chalkboard hard, as if it would magically give them the answers they needed.

'Could we ask this Urcu dude to do his magic on Levi?' Ezra asked.

Levi shook his head wildly. 'Na-uh, nope. No humans can talk to Urcuchillay. He's got the magic that turns llamas into toy llamas and vice versa. He don't take requests from anyone but Mama Llama.'

'How does Mama Llama make a request?' Yasmin questioned.

'No one knows for sure apart from the head guys in SNH. But my mate said there's a set of magic spells...' Levi narrowed his eyes as if they might be overheard by unseen ears.

Yasmin's face lit up. 'A magic spell? Even if there's a small chance it exists, we have to find it and do it!'

'Definitely!' Ezra agreed.

Levi huffed and kicked his back legs. He did that when he was thinking hard.

'I guess, I've got nothing left to lose ... All right, I'm in too. But we'd have to go to the London paddock. If anyone's got a copy of those mysterious magic spells, it's Travis.'

Yasmin looked at her chalkboard, her mind already filling it with even more plans.

'We're going to break into Seen Not Herd HQ!'

CHAPTER FOURTEEN
The Mission Kicks Off

DISCLAIMER: I must warn you, reader, that breaking and entering a property under any circumstances (even if it's to find a magic llama spell) is ILLEGAL and therefore BAD.

Yasmin and Ezra were aware of this, of course, so they chose to sneak into the HQ while it was open in the day.

Sneaking = okay.

Breaking in = NOPE.

It has to be said, though, that Levi didn't really care either way.

There was a chill in the air on the fateful September morn when Yasmin and Levi crept to the front door

148

dressed head to toe in black. Yasmin wore a black turtleneck, black trousers and a black beanie. Levi had donned his *Men in Black* (or *Llama in Black*) suit again with the earpiece now connected to Yasmin's phone for communication. They were dressed for creeping around in the shadows and, luckily for them, it was a particularly dark and dreary Sunday.

Yasmin silently opened the front door, quickly shouting a brief 'Bye!' before rushing out of the house with Levi. She was trying to avoid having to answer too many questions about where she was going dressed like a cat burglar and why. Yasmin had told her ammi earlier that morning she was meeting Gilly at OLD and, even though she was still in her parents' bad books, they agreed as they considered it 'community engagement' and therefore educational. And Yasmin *was* going to meet up with Gilly.

Just . . . after she'd pulled off a llama heist. That's all.

At the end of Fish Lane Yasmin could see Ezra waiting for them on the corner as agreed. But there was something off about him . . .

'What is that boy wearing?' Levi said, squinting as he trotted along beside Yasmin.

As they got closer, it was clear Ezra hadn't got the memo about 'blending into your surroundings'.

'Uh, Ezra, what's that you've got on?' Yasmin asked, stifling a giggle.

'I don't have any black clothes,' Ezra explained. 'This is all I could find.'

Ezra was dressed in a Halloween bat onesie with wings attached to the arms and everything.

'We're supposed to be super-slick secret agents, mate!' Levi guffawed, circling Ezra to take in the whole look. 'Don't you think this might draw a bit of attention?'

Ezra blushed and Yasmin felt sorry for him.

'It doesn't matter. It's black anyway. Come on, let's go!'

So the Llama-in-black, the cat burglar and the bat set off down Brick Lane, following Levi's instructions towards the London paddock.

Rounding the corner of yet another thin and windy cobbled road, Levi pointed to a building. 'That's it. Right there.'

They'd only been walking about fifteen minutes

and they hadn't even needed to get a bus. Yasmin had thought that the London paddock would be somewhere like Westminster or on the bank of the River Thames next to MI6. Instead, they were on an empty road in East London called Olde Butt Lane.

Ezra couldn't contain his laughter at the street name and had to sit down for a while to regain his composure. He even took a selfie next to it.

'I'm going to send it to my grandpa in Jamaica; he's gonna love this,' he said, wiping the tears from his eyes.

Yasmin clapped her hands together. 'Okay, focus. Take it seriously, Ezra! We have one shot at doing this. Levi, which building is it?'

Levi pointed at a tall building at the end of a row of terraces. It had a white-stone facade and a glowing sign in the window that said 'Sushi'. The big window took up most of the shopfront and they could see tables inside where people were eating. There was an alleyway running alongside it that led to a dead end filled with rubbish bins.

'Uhhh, Levi, that looks like a sushi bar.' Yasmin wasn't convinced this was the right spot.

'It's actually a sushi bar slash coffee shop slash yoga studio slash office space,' Levi corrected her, already walking ahead. 'It used to be a chippy but then the hipsters found it and you know the rest!' He rolled his eyes dramatically.

'So Seen Not Herd HQ is . . . in there?' Ezra questioned, following Yasmin with his bat wings blowing in the breeze.

'Apparently,' Yasmin answered, shrugging her shoulders.

'Yeah, round the back in the old storeroom.' Levi continued. 'No one goes in there cos the only door in or out is locked. The door leads to the alleyway.'

Yasmin stopped abruptly. 'So how will we get in?'

Levi swung his head round and looked at both Yasmin and Ezra with a smirk.

'I've got that covered. Follow me.'

This is our ticket into the London paddock.

Yasmin peered down through the gaps in the metal grate and into a different world.

What Levi had described as an old storeroom was actually a complex high-tech operation centre, which was clad in metal from ceiling to floor with tables holding computers, equipment and paperwork. At the front of the room was a wall entirely made of LED screens showing locations around the UK and a radar emitting a regular beeping noise.

But, best of all, and weirdest of all . . . the room was populated by toy llamas.

There were black-furred llamas.

Sandy-coloured llamas.

Llamas with spectacles.

Llamas wearing shirts.

A llama fixing a tiny motorbike.

A llama photocopying.

Even a llama doing target practice with cocktail sticks instead of javelins.

It was a llama metropolis. A llamopolis, if you prefer.

Yasmin and Ezra looked at each other, their eyes wide in wonder. 'Cooooool,' they whispered in unison.

Yasmin leaned further down towards the grate and put her eye right up to the hole.

'If I was a magic spell where would I be?' she mused, scanning the room for clues.

Her gaze fell on a familiar llama sitting at the biggest desk with his feet up and drinking coffee from a tiny paper cup.

'Ugh, Travis. And he's not even using a reusable mug,' Yasmin reported back to Ezra and Levi.

Levi tutted. 'Typical. What's he doing?'

Yasmin watched for a few moments. 'Nothing really. He's just bossing the other llamas around.'

'Uh, I hate bossy people,' Ezra chipped in. His concentration was wearing thin from all the watching and waiting, so he'd got up to start rummaging through the boxes around them.

Yasmin kept watching Travis intently until he took his legs down off the table and stood up.

'Right, everyone, team lunch meeting. There's a *lot* to discuss about Manchester quadrant four this week.' Travis picked up some files off his table and went into an adjoining room to a chorus of groans. Seems like the other llamas weren't a fan of lunchtime meetings.

But then Yasmin spotted something. Where Travis had removed some files off his desk, a folder was lying underneath. A folder marked 'Transformations'.

'There, there, I've found it!' Yasmin whispered excitedly. 'There's a folder on his desk about transformations. I bet that can tell us how to keep you as a real llama forever.'

Levi breathed out a heavy sigh. 'This is definitely against the rules of SNH. And I'm sure Urcuchillay won't be pleased. Plus, if Travis sees me, he will lock me up!'

'Travis won't see you if we're quick and I'm sure Urcuchillay will understand,' Yasmin reasoned. 'Levi, they've all gone to lunch. It's our only chance to get that folder.'

Levi straightened himself up and puffed out his chest. 'You're right. I'll go. If anyone's gonna get caught, it should be me.'

Yasmin looked down at the room below. It was a long way and even if Levi got down there, he wouldn't be able to get out of the locked door. 'It's too far for you to climb back up here afterwards. How are you going to escape?'

'How about this?' Ezra asked. From the box he had investigated he pulled out a long rubber band with a handle at each end. 'I think it's for yoga. My mum uses one to stretch.'

Yasmin beamed. 'Ezra, that's a great idea.'

Working quickly, they tied one end of the rubber band round Levi's waist.

'Ooof, that's tight,' he complained, pulling at the band. 'I knew I should have laid off all those bagels recently.'

Then Ezra and Yasmin carefully lifted the metal grate, trying to make as little noise as possible. It was deadly silent in the room below now that all the llamas had gone, apart from the steady beeping of the radar.

Slowly and steadily Yasmin lowered Levi into the room, stopping abruptly at the smallest sound for fear someone would come in and see Levi hovering five feet above Travis's desk. Yasmin's heart was beating hard and she was so nervous her hands were sweaty. At the next lowering of the band her hand slipped and Levi plummeted a few inches.

'Whoa!' Ezra caught the end of the band just in time, preventing Levi from banging into one of the motorbikes.

'Sorry,' Yasmin whispered.

They kept lowering Levi bit by bit, until he was finally close enough to reach the folder.

'Where did you leave it, Travis? On your desk?' came a voice from the meeting-room door, which had just opened.

Someone was coming!

In a blind panic Yasmin and Ezra pulled up the exercise band as fast as they could, with Levi swinging wildly from side to side. But he hadn't managed to grab the folder yet. They'd have to wait it out until the llama left.

The llama from the meeting trotted over to Travis's desk and paused.

Yasmin, Ezra and Levi all held their breath, hoping that by some miracle the llama would not look up and see Levi dangling directly above it.

The llama collected up some loose papers and lifted its head *just* a smidge.

It was going to look up.

It was going to see Levi.

A second passed, which felt like an eternity, then the llama shuffled the papers, turned and went back to the meeting room, shutting the door behind it.

Yasmin, Ezra and Levi let out a collective sigh of relief.

'Right, let's get this folder and go,' Yasmin whispered. They lowered Levi once more, who this time grabbed the folder, plus a few chocolate digestives Travis had on his desk, before being winched back up to safety.

As Yasmin replaced the grate Levi jumped up and down waving the folder in the air. 'We got it! Oh my god, that was sick!'

'Let's read it now!' Ezra said, beaming and taking the folder from Levi.

'No, we've gotta get out fast.' Yasmin kept her

voice low. 'As soon as they realise the folder is missing they'll know somebody took it. They'll probably even call Mama Llama to get on the case. We should take it home where it's safe.'

Levi and Ezra nodded, though they looked a little disappointed.

The trio snuck back down the stairs from the attic, through the now empty yoga studio, down the next flight of wooden stairs, through the cafe space, out of the kitchen and back into the alley.

As they stepped out into the cold air, Yasmin breathed for what felt like the first time since they had got there. The cool breeze felt good on her flushed cheeks and sweaty palms. They'd made it in and out, and they had the folder. 'Let's get home,' she said and smiled.

They started walking back towards the road and they'd just reached the top of the alley when –

'HEY, YOU! STOP!'

Yasmin, Ezra and Levi whirled round to see three

bulky grey llamas on motorbikes spilling out of the building into the alley.

Yasmin scooped up Levi and turned to Ezra. 'Run!!!!!!'

CHAPTER SIXTEEN
Pursued by Llamas

The whirring sound of three tiny motorbike engines buzzed in Yasmin's ears as she legged it down the back streets of Shoreditch, Ezra beside her. Their feet pounded the hard cobblestones and sent echoes down the empty streets as they ran, ran, ran.

'Are they close?' Yasmin panted through ragged breaths.

'They're catching up. Those bikes must've been upgraded to double-A batteries!' Levi reported back. He was gripping Yasmin's shoulders but facing backwards, trying to tell them which way their llama pursuers were heading.

'We have to lose them!' Ezra shouted, still gripping the folder that had got them into this mess. 'This way!'

166

They turned right and headed into a park and across a basketball court. It was raining now, meaning no one was out playing, but the ground was slippery, which slowed the bikes down. If there had been more people around, the llamas wouldn't have been able to be out in public. Where was everyone when you were being pursued by llamas?!

'Across this bump!' Ezra called, gesturing to the skate ramp they'd played on so many times that summer. Surely the llamas' bikes wouldn't be powerful enough to make it up the steep ramp?

Yasmin and Ezra ran over the bump and took a second on the other side to catch their breath. There was a moment when the engines seemed to falter. Maybe the llamas had given up?

But then, out of nowhere, three small black motorbikes and their llama riders came shooting over the ramp, flying high into the air. It seemed as if they floated in slow motion as Yasmin watched, amazed, at the llamas soaring through the sky and

landing the bikes in perfect formation.

'Go, go, go!' Levi yelled, and they took off again, running through the park as fast as they could.

The streets on the other side of the park seemed busier and Yasmin had an idea.

'Head for those streets – they can't be seen moving around in public!'

Ezra followed her and the bikes whirred on furiously behind.

'We might make it!' Yasmin panted.

Ezra started laughing. 'This is actually quite fun –
WHOA.'

While Ezra was laughing, he had lost concentration
and nearly crashed into a bin. He tried to move out
of the way but the grass was wet and he skidded a
good few feet before tumbling to the ground. The
folder flew out of his hands and landed in the lap of
the biggest, burliest toy llama.

'Hey, thanks,' it said, smirking and tucking the folder away in the seat of the motorbike. 'Guys? Let's get this back to HQ.'

The llamas revved their engines and sped away into the distance, taking the folder and any chance of Levi staying a toy llama in London with them.

The rain had started pouring down now, soaking Yasmin through to her socks. She watched the bikes as they disappeared out of view and carried on staring long after they were gone. All that work to sneak into HQ and get the folder had been for nothing.

She turned slowly back to look at Ezra who was getting up, covered in mud.

'Guess I'm going to need a shower when I get home. Sorry, Yasmin.' He chuckled sheepishly, trying to ease the tension.

Levi was still clinging to Yasmin's shoulder, getting drenched right into his stuffing. She took off her hat and put it over him before turning to Ezra.

'What happened?' she said coolly.

'I slipped. I tried to hold on to the folder but I guess I just lost my grip,' Ezra explained.

'You weren't looking where you were going,' Yasmin said through gritted teeth.

'Yassy, it's okay, love.' Levi patted her shoulder.

'No it isn't!' She turned to Ezra. 'You were laughing; that's why you didn't see the bin. Don't you realise this is important?'

Ezra looked confused. 'I know it's important. I–'

'You don't!' Yasmin yelled, her tears mixing with the rain that streamed down her face. 'Levi is my guardian and now he's leaving. That folder was our last chance and you ruined it! Why can't you take this seriously? This is more important than having fun! I need him.'

'No, you don't,' Ezra said quietly.

'Yes, I do! You don't know anything about me! I wish I'd never told you about Levi.' Yasmin wasn't thinking about what she was saying any more. It was just coming out. She was sure this wasn't good communication but she didn't care.

Ezra wiped mud from his face and looked at Yasmin with a trembling lip. 'If you can't say anything nice, Yasmin, then maybe you shouldn't speak at all.' Then he turned and ran away across the park, not looking back.

'You didn't mean those things, Yassy . . .' Levi whispered in her ear. 'Go and say sorry.'

Yasmin shook her head. 'No. He's right. I shouldn't speak at all.'

Slowly Yasmin sloshed through the wet, muddy grass until she reached the other side of the park. Brick Lane stretched out in front of her, the little shopfronts lit up in the darkening afternoon. She thought back to when Levi first came into her life. About how she'd gone up and down this street finding ways to get rid of him so she could stay quiet and unheard. Without Levi she'd never have learned to talk, never have made a friend in Ezra . . . She'd never have been brave.

Walking on autopilot, she made her way down the street, past the fish market and up to the front door of a familiar building. She knocked once and waited for the door to swing open.

Mr Matthews, the group leader of OLD answered the door. 'Yasmin, my god, you're soaking. Um, would you mind taking your shoes off at the entrance? We've just had the carpet cleaned.'

Yasmin nodded and slipped off her sodden shoes. As she took off her wet jumper and hung it over the radiator, she realised that Levi wasn't on her shoulder any more. He'd probably gone off to try to find Ezra – or, more likely, to get warm and have a hot chocolate at her house.

Still dripping muddy water from the bottom of her trousers, Yasmin trudged into the main seating area where the members of OLD openly stared at her. They loved a bit of drama and this had intrigue written all over it.

'Oh my word, Yasmin, you look like a drowned rat.' Gilly heaved herself up from her favourite armchair.

As soon as Yasmin saw Gilly's familiar multicoloured knitted clothes and tie-dye cardigan she burst into tears again.

'Ohhhh no, what's wrong?' Gilly ushered Yasmin into a corner of the room, away from the prying eyes of the other members who audibly let out disappointed sighs.

Yasmin got out her phone and wrote a message, then showed it to Gilly.

Can I type instead? Don't feel like talking.

'Of course,' Gilly responded, stroking Yasmin's wet hair. 'Fire away.'

I had a fight with Ezra. I said mean things to him and –

Yasmin suddenly realised she could only tell Gilly one tiny part of the story. She couldn't mention anything about Levi. That's why she'd shared the secret in the first place, so she could have someone to talk to about it. And now she'd gone and told Ezra she wished she'd never told him . . . Yasmin deleted the 'and' at the end of the message and showed Gilly.

Gilly raised her eyebrows. 'Uh-oh, a fight. How mean were you?'

Very.

'Then why don't you just go and say sorry?' Gilly suggested, her voice gentle.

I don't know how. Every time I speak it goes wrong. I had a big fight with a girl at school too. I can't keep things in my head any more without blurting them out. I thought now that I talk it would be easy to get along with other kids but it's impossible!

Gilly grabbed her glasses to read this one. She took her time and then thought about it for a while, pursing her lips, which she'd painted bright purple.

'Well, it seems to me that you're being hard on yourself,' Gilly said finally.

Yasmin was shocked. Had Gilly read what she'd just typed? She'd been mean to two people!

'You didn't speak from when you were a toddler until just a few months ago, right?' Gilly asked.

Yasmin nodded.

'So you haven't had much practice! You aren't going to be perfect at speaking to people immediately. It's about listening, which you're already good at, but also talking to people in a way that they understand.' Gilly stopped. 'Does that make sense?'

Do you mean communicating?

'Yes!' Gilly clapped her hands together. 'It's hard, Yasmin, and people learn how to do it over their whole life. Some people never learn how to communicate . . .' Gilly glared at Mr Matthews across the room. 'He's so rude; always using my oat milk without asking.'

Yasmin giggled. She felt a little better and was ready to talk again. She coughed a little to clear her throat before she spoke.

'I still can't communicate with Ammi and Papa. But

maybe that's because I haven't had much practice in talking to them . . .'

'Maybe,' Gilly agreed.

'But I do have a lot of practice of *showing* them what I mean. Before I spoke I guess I had to find other ways of communicating. Maybe I could do that now with art club. Show them why it's important rather than tell them?'

Gilly whistled, impressed. 'Well, Yasmin, I might be eighty-five but you seem like the wise one here.'

Yasmin gave Gilly one more big squeeze, gathered up her damp clothes and left OLD. It was still drizzling but Yasmin was already soggy so she headed out into the streets. Gilly's advice went round and round her head as she walked. Talking seemed to carry a lot of responsibility, but was it worth it?

At least she knew the best way to *show* her parents how much art meant to her – by finishing her comic. Hopefully Levi would be home too so they could spend one last evening together eating biscuits and watching TV. Yasmin felt a deep pang in her chest. *LOUDMOUTH* had been inspired by him: their adventure together and the fun (and chaos) he had brought to her life. With him gone ... what would she even draw?

Yasmin finally got home and let herself in, only to be met at the door by Papa.

'Oh, Yasmin, you've been out in the rain?' Papa seemed worried. 'You'll get ill. Go and change quickly.'

'YOUCAN'TBEPOORLYYASMIN,' Ammi shouted over her shoulder, stirring a huge pot of minced lamb and tomatoes. 'NOMISSINGSCHOOL.'

Yasmin nodded and trudged up the stairs, leaving damp footprints behind her.

When she got to her room it was dark inside.

'Levi?' she said in a quiet and croaky voice. 'Levi, where are you?'

She flicked the lights on and scanned the room, panic rising in her chest. She flipped over her pillows and lifted the duvet, but there was no sign of him.

She flung open the wardrobe and rummaged through the contents too, but he wasn't there either.

Then something caught her eye, or rather, the absence of something made her run over to her desk. Her *LOUDMOUTH* comic was gone! All the work she'd done that summer had just disappeared.

Something was going on, but there were too many questions swimming around in Yasmin's head to piece it together. In a haze she collapsed on to the bed, shivering. First things first, she needed to change into some dry clothes.

It was while Yasmin was sourcing her biggest, warmest jumper that she heard the phone ring and Ammi's voice booming up the stairs.

'NO EZRA ISN'T HERE. YASMIN GOT HOME FIFTEEN MINUTES AGO. I HOPE YOU FIND HIM.'

Levi was missing.

LOUDMOUTH was missing.

Ezra was missing.

And Yasmin knew they were all connected.

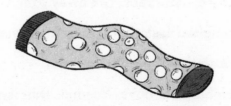

CHAPTER EIGHTEEN
The Final Judgement

As soon as Yasmin came down the stairs, her parents and aunties surrounded her.

'EZRAISMISSING!'

'I've already rung round all the aunties in the area.'

'We've got eyes all over Whitechapel.'

Her brothers were sitting at the kitchen table eating their second dinner of the evening.

'Well done, Yasmin. The only friend you've ever had and you lost him,' Tall Brother said in between slurps of daal.

'He's probably run away from you!' Short Brother laughed before Papa gently whacked the back of both their heads.

'Stop it, boys. Yasmin, this is serious - do you know where he is?' Papa drew himself up and commanded the room with his best 'I'm the man of the house' voice.

Yasmin waited for the questions to die down before she spoke.

'It's okay. I think I know where he is.'

Papa nodded, pulling on his coat. 'Okay, good, we'll come with you. Sisters, stay here and watch the boys.'

The aunties pouted, annoyed to miss out, but agreed to stay. They'd find a way to get all the details later anyway – they always managed to.

Ammi tied her headscarf, gathered her enormous handbag and put on her warm coat. (She still wore her sandals, though; Yasmin had even seen her go out in the snow with them once.)

Yasmin figured that Ezra needed somewhere to think and he found it easiest to concentrate when he was on the drums. Her best guess was that they'd find him in the music room at school. At least she really hoped so.

Ammi, Papa and Yasmin caught the bus two stops to Fish Lane Primary, spending the short journey in silence. Ammi texted Ezra's mum to let her know they were checking the school and would call with any updates. Her face was lined with worry as she typed and Yasmin realised for the first time how fond Ammi was of Ezra.

Papa led them off the bus and strode up to the front gate of the school, pushing the buzzer with authority. After a little wait, the caretaker's voice came crackling through the intercom. 'Hello, you got a delivery?'

'No, I am a parent. I believe there's a child here in the music room,' Papa said confidently.

'Impossible. School's closed today to kids. Only a couple of staff in for training. That's why I'm here *on a Sunday*,' the caretaker said in a gruff voice.

'Well, there's a child missing and we'd like to check. Better safe than sorry, hmm?' Papa replied curtly.

There was a short pause and then the gate buzzed open.

Yasmin looked at her papa with admiration. He definitely had no problem with communicating what he wanted. She grabbed his hand as they walked in.

'The music room's this way.' Yasmin started to lead her parents to the back of the school. But, as they passed reception, she noticed a sign stuck to the wall.

Yasmin's eyes narrowed . . . She recognised that wonky handwriting, and there was only one llama she knew who couldn't resist a fart joke. This glimmer of hope gave Yasmin a spring to her step.

'Actually, let's go this way,' she instructed her parents. They followed the sign and walked all the way down the corridor that led to the left of the school building, past empty classrooms and coat pegs holding forgotten jumpers. Once they reached the end of the corridor there was yet another sign with an arrow pasted to the wall, pointing up to the first floor. So up the stairs they went, across scratchy-carpeted corridors lined with examples of students' work until they reached the art rooms.

In one of the rooms Yasmin could hear activity and a familiar voice. With caution she reached out and gently pushed the door open. But she could never have been prepared for what she saw inside.

'Oh my gosh . . .' Yasmin let go of Papa's hand and wandered inside.

'EZRAYOUARESAFE!' Ammi rushed forward and squeezed Ezra to her chest. 'IWILLRINGYOUR MUMSTRAIGHTAWAY.'

'What is this?' Papa asked no one in particular, looking around at all the pictures.

'Well, it isn't finished yet!' Ezra replied shyly once Ammi had released him.

On the walls of the art room, Ezra and Levi had

pasted huge photocopies of pages from *LOUDMOUTH*. There was the page that showed the main character, Jasmine, finding the alpaca, Leroy, in her cupboard. The page where she was playing a dramatic chess match. The page where Jasmine and Leroy reunite at the farm . . .

Ammi finished telling Ezra's mum he was safe and strode back into the room, slowing down when she saw the pictures. She and Papa moved around, looking at all the pictures intensely, chuckling at some and pointing out bits they liked. Yasmin watched them, holding her breath and letting her art speak for her.

Finally, Ammi and Papa turned to her and Yasmin was relieved to see they were smiling.

'I'd recognise my daughter's artwork anywhere,' Papa said proudly. 'You get your creative talent from me.'

'ANDME.' Ammi poked him in the ribs. 'THISONEISMYFAVOURITE.' She stood in front of

a picture from the end of *LOUDMOUTH*. It was of Jasmine hugging her mum and dad in front of the alpaca at the farm.

Yasmin picked up the full comic that was lying on one of the tables and held it out to her parents. 'This is what I really want to do. It makes me happy and calm. Plus, I think I'm good at it. I was even going to enter a competition but . . . I missed the deadline.'

Ammi furrowed her brow. 'WHYDIDN'TYOU TELLUS?'

'Well, I did, kind of. But it was in the middle of you telling me off. Plus, you were so focused on the science team and I want you to be proud of me. I didn't think I could ask you to let me do art instead.'

Papa and Ammi gave each other a look that Yasmin could not decipher. It was one of those looks your parents share when they somehow magically know what the other is thinking.

Papa finally broke the silence. 'You know, jaan, your brothers are always asking for things. Games, trainers . . . you can ask us for things too. Within reason.'

Yasmin smiled. 'Thank you. I'm learning.'

'WEAREN'TSCARYMONSTERS,' Ammi joked. 'WELOVEYOU.'

Yasmin giggled. 'You are a little bit scary.'

Papa looked around the room again at Ezra and Levi's makeshift art show.

'Yasmin, you are a talented artist *and* a talented scientist. We are very proud.'

'MYDAUGHTERISMULTITALENTED!' Ammi agreed, stroking Yasmin's head. And Yasmin knew she'd be saying the same thing to her friend Nasreen on the phone later that night.

Then Ammi turned to Ezra, speaking for once in a normal volume. 'You did this all yourself for Yasmin?

You are a good friend. But a naughty boy for worrying your parents!'

She wagged her finger but Yasmin could see she was still smiling.

Ezra shrugged. 'That's what friends do.'

'Yassy, Ezra's parents are downstairs. We're going to go explain to them what happened,' Papa explained. 'Hopefully we'll get you out of too much trouble.'

Ammi and Papa hurried out of the room with Ammi yelling, 'STAYHERE,' as they left.

Yasmin felt absolutely terrible for the type of friend she'd been to Ezra. She picked up Levi, who had become inanimate the moment her parents had come into the room and looked at Ezra guiltily.

'Ezra, I am so, so, so sorry times a million. I was mean to you because I was sad about Levi.' Yasmin looked down at Levi who was gazing back up at her with big shiny eyes.

'I know . . . Levi told me you were sorry. But I

should say sorry too. I did lose focus when we were running; it's my fault we lost the folder.' Ezra fidgeted with his top awkwardly and Yasmin realised he was still wearing his bat costume. Despite everything that had happened, she couldn't help but burst out laughing and pretty soon Ezra and Levi were laughing too.

'Thank you so much for doing this for me,' Yasmin said, looking around the room again.

'It was Levi's idea,' Ezra explained. 'He told me he needed my help cos he doesn't have opposable thumbs. I thought it was a great way to show *everyone* how good your art is.'

'But how did you understand him?' Yasmin cocked her head to one side.

'Telepathy,' Levi announced.

Yasmin's mouth dropped open.

'Nah, only joking. I sent him a text.' Levi winked. 'I wanted to do one last thing for ya, Yasmin, so you could see how talented you are with ya drawings.

You don't need me. I realised you've always been much better at showing than telling. Maybe that's your way of communicating?'

Yasmin held Levi up to her face and squeezed him tight. 'You're the best llama guardian in the world.'

'I'll be the judge of that,' came a smooth voice from behind them.

It was Mama Llama. And she was glorious.

She was wearing a long shiny black trench coat with red pointed glasses and lipstick of such a vibrant red Yasmin was sure her aunties would approve.

'Mama Llama,' Yasmin, Ezra and Levi breathed in awe.

'Correct.' Mama Llama strode forward. 'And I have some business to attend to with all of you.'

Yasmin noticed that Mama Llama walked on her back two legs like a human. A definite power move.

'In all my forty years in this job I've never seen an

agent and a *child* disregard the rules so totally.' Mama Llama clip-clopped closer.

'Mama Llama, may I just say you look great for forty years on the job?' Levi interrupted.

Mama Llama tossed back her curly hair. 'I know. But that's beside the point. Together you have broken exactly one hundred and six rules in the Seen Not Herd rule book.'

Ezra tapped Yasmin on the shoulder. 'What's she saying? She looks angry.'

'She is,' Yasmin whispered back. She brought up her phone so she could type out what Mama Llama was saying for Ezra to see. It took a lot of brain power and concentration and Yasmin wished he could hear them too.

'Agent Levi, you are hereby revoked of your llama licence,' Mama Llama announced. 'As you for, Yasmin Shah . . .'

Yasmin's stomach dropped. She'd never been so afraid of something four times her miniature before.

'We in upper management at Seen Not Herd have no idea why you can hear all of us llamas. Usually a child can hear their guardian and that's it. Perhaps Agent Levi did such a terrible job that he confused the magic that created him in the first place.' Mama Llama tapped her foot against the floor.

'Wait a second.' Yasmin placed Levi down on the table in front of her. 'If this is it and you're leaving forever, then I want you to hear something. You too, Mama Llama.'

Mama Llama huffed in irritation, but she gestured for Yasmin to go on.

'Levi, it's no secret that when you first appeared we didn't exactly get along . . .'

'She threw me in the rubbish truck,' Levi laughed, reminiscing.

'But once I realised what you were doing . . . trying to get me to stand up for myself. You did help me. You annoyed me into speaking for the first time in seven years – doesn't that count for something? You encouraged me to make friends with kids my own age.'

Ezra smiled. 'Hey, that's me!'

'And even though you are the loudest, most irritating prankster llama I've ever met, you're my friend and the first person who really heard me. Look at what you did for me.' Yasmin gazed around the room filled with her artwork. 'Thank you.'

Levi jumped up into Yasmin's arms and they had a huge hug.

'Ew, Levi, you've got snot all over my jumper.'

Levi sniffed. 'I'm sorry, but that was such a beautiful speech.'

'Um, guys . . . look,' Ezra whispered, pointing at Mama Llama.

Yasmin blinked hard . . . It looked like Mama Llama was crying too!

'Oh, um, excuse me,' she said, dabbing at her eyes with a silk hanky. 'Yasmin . . . that speech . . .

well. You *communicated* your point very well.'

Yasmin smiled.
'Thanks.'

'Agent Levi –'
Mama Llama turned
to him – 'your
methods are highly
unorthodox and
reckless. However . . .
you're obviously
doing something
right. I can't believe
I'm saying this, but
let me take your case
back to the board.
Perhaps there is
something that can

be done to preserve your position here with
Yasmin.'

Levi jumped up and clicked his heels together

in glee. 'I thought I was done for! Thank you, thank you!'

Even Ezra jumped up and down, before he gave Yasmin a big hug.

Yasmin stood in shock, a grin slowly spreading on her face. Could this really be happening? Was Levi safe?

'I'll get back to you with the board's decision as soon as possible,' Mama Llama said, composing herself. 'Until then, *please* stay out of trouble. That includes breaking into and entering our headquarters, hmm?'

All three of them fell silent and looked at the floor sheepishly.

'Um, with all due respect . . . we were actually just sneaking in . . .' Levi mumbled.

Mama Llama raised a single unimpressed eyebrow and hopped up on to the ledge of the open window. 'You'll be hearing from me.'

With that she leaped into the air and took off

across the rooftops, bouncing and flipping parkour-style into the horizon.

Ezra watched in awe. 'Whoa . . . she's sick.'

Levi was safe for now. Now all they could do was wait.

CHAPTER NINETEEN
LOUDMOUTH

There are a few tried and tested ways of passing the time when you're waiting for the results of an important test.

1. Pace up and down the house until you get dizzy.

2. Eat a multipack of crisps and a family-size bar of chocolate.

3. Annoy your siblings until your parents send you out of the house.

Yasmin had tried all these at least twice while they waited for Mama Llama to get back to them. Her pacing had even started to annoy Levi, which was definitely a first.

'Come on, Yassy – we gotta get out of the house. You're going mad up here. It's been a week!' Levi tugged on Yasmin's sleeve with his mouth, trying to lead her to the bedroom door.

'But what if Mama Llama comes here looking for you?' Yasmin whined, looking out of the window.

'She can reach me on my llama landline. Now get a move on. It's Saturday and usually kids have *fun*. Remember what fun is? I told Ezra to meet us at the skatepark.' Levi waited by the door until Yasmin reluctantly picked up her coat and put on her trainers.

The skatepark was empty apart for Ezra who was whizzing up and over a bump when Yasmin and Levi got there. Luckily, it was a dry day and there was piercing sunlight despite the chill in the air. Yasmin raised her hand and waved as they got close and Ezra waved back.

'Yasmin, look at this!' he called, flicking his skateboard into the air under his feet and landing back on it.

'Yes, you finally got it!' Yasmin gave him a high- five.

'And did you finish *LOUDMOUTH*? Oh, and have your parents made a decision about science team?' Ezra asked eagerly.

Ammi and Papa had told Yasmin they needed a few days to make a decision about whether she could leave the science team and go to art club instead. Yasmin had used the time wisely, working on her comic after school every day. Even though she'd missed the deadline for the *Comic Action* competition, she thought having her very own exhibition hosted by her friends was an even better prize.

Levi rummaged in Yasmin's rucksack and brought out the finished comic, fully shaded in and even laminated by Papa. Ezra flicked through it happily as Yasmin explained her parents' final decision.

'They're letting me do art club *as long* as I keep up my A grades in science,' Yasmin explained. 'Levi helped me negotiate the terms.'

'It's all about giving them an offer they can't refuse,' said Levi. 'Yasmin's parents can't get enough of A grades.'

Yasmin giggled. It was true. There was something she hadn't taken Levi's advice on, though. Earlier in the week, Yasmin had gone up to Tia at lunchtime and apologised for being a birthday ruiner. Levi had told her not to – that Tia was a bully so she didn't deserve it. But Yasmin disagreed. Everyone deserved to be the winner on their birthday. At least Tia got to be a winner at the science tournament. She and Remi had taken on Oakmead again and won, three against two! Miss Zainab had insisted on hosting at their school after Mr Johnson's dodgy behaviour at the heats, so there was no funny business.

Ezra and Yasmin practised kickflips for a while until they needed a break. They were all sitting at the top of one of the skate ramps, sharing a box of raisins, when a small figure appeared opposite them on a skateboard.

It dropped down the ramp, soared up into the air, did a 360-degree flip and landed right next to them.

'Is there anything you can't do?' Levi yelled, his eyes wide in amazement.

'Not really,' Mama Llama replied, taking off her

helmet. 'I'm glad I found you. I went to your house but no one was there.'

'I told you!' Yasmin protested but Levi shushed her.

'I have news,' Mama Llama announced. 'The board has discussed your licence, Levi, and we have decided to make your role as Yasmin's guardian permanent.'

Yasmin and Levi cheered, followed a few seconds later by Ezra who worked out what must have happened.

'We've also had some interesting news about you, Yasmin. You see, as the head of Seen Not Herd, I am the only llama allowed to communicate with Urcuchillay, the llama god responsible for choosing the real llamas that will become toy guardians. It seems that over the course of your friendship, you have helped Levi just as much as he's helped you.'

Levi nodded. 'Makes sense. I was a mess before you, Yasmin.'

'As such, you are also his guardian as he is yours. This is why you are able to hear all the llamas. Because of this, Urcuchillay, god of the llamas, creator of all guardian llamas has deemed you, Yasmin Shah . . .'

She paused for dramatic effect. Yasmin waited, her heart thumping, wondering what on earth Mama Llama was going to say.

'An honorary guardian llama!'

Yasmin fell off the side of the skate ramp.

'What happened?' Ezra asked, jumping down to help Yasmin back up.

'I'm – I'm a . . . guardian llama too?' Yasmin stammered.

'An *honorary* guardian llama. So you should be very *honoured*,' Mama Llama continued. 'There is a full moon tonight, during which your statuses as guardian llamas will be made permanent. I'm glad this could be resolved.' Mama Llama started to put her helmet back on.

'Wait, what did she say?' Ezra asked again. Seeing the confusion on Ezra's face, something that Yasmin had wanted for a while played on her mind. She decided to test her communication skills once more and just prayed the timing was right.

'Mama Llama, I have a request. Please could you ask Urcuchillay tonight to grant Ezra permission to hear Levi too? I am honoured, of course, but being an honorary guardian llama isn't the same unless I can share the adventure with my best friend.' Yasmin grabbed Ezra's hand and squeezed.

Mama Llama sighed and shook her head. 'I'll ask. But I can't make any promises. Is that everything?'

Yasmin and Levi nodded eagerly and Mama Llama skated back off into the horizon.

'Yasmin, you didn't have to do that for me,' Ezra said, 'but it would be cool to be able to hear Levi.'

Yasmin chuckled. 'I did it for me too. Do you know how annoying it is being a llama translator? Plus, how can I get better at communication if you don't know what's going on?'

'So what happens at midnight under the moon? Is there a spell we have to do?' Ezra asked looking up the sky.

Levi shook his head firmly. 'I cannot divulge that information. It's a sacred llama tradition. But let's just say it involves some candles, some chanting and some hay.'

As they were getting hungry, Yasmin, Ezra and

Levi left the skatepark to go back to Yasmin's house. They'd asked for a sleepover, so it was lucky that they could be together to see if their request would be granted by Urcuchillay.

Ammi and Papa had prepared a delicious dinner and all seven members of Yasmin's family, plus Ezra, sat round the table to eat. There were chapattis, a squash curry, lamb samosas and fragrant rice, which Ezra had double helpings of.

'What do you enjoy at school then, Ezra?' Auntie Gigi asked when they were having chai after dinner.

'I love music. I play the drums,' Ezra answered politely.

'Wow, the drums are cool!' Short Brother said before Tall Brother nudged him to be quiet. Calling anything cool was definitely not cool according to her brothers.

Once dinner was finished and the washing-up had been done, Ezra and Yasmin were allowed to go up to her bedroom. Levi was sitting on the bed already, reading his *Llamas of London* magazine and munching on a samosa he'd managed to pinch.

'Good dinner?' he said through big bites.

'Delicious!' Ezra rubbed his belly as he got into his sleeping bag on the camp bed. 'Your family makes the best food.'

Yasmin grinned, feeling proud. Her family did have some perks.

Settling down to bed, Yasmin turned off the lights and Levi curled up beside her.

'How will we know if the spell works?' Yasmin asked into the dark room.

'I guess we'll find out in the morning, if I can hear Levi,' Ezra pondered. 'But don't worry, Yasmin. Even if I can't, we'll find a way to communicate. We did before when you didn't speak.'

'That's true. Maybe we should try and stay up all night?' Yasmin suggested.

'Yeah, okay!' Ezra answered. 'Let's play our game, "What would you rather be?"'

Yasmin and Ezra had made this game up one particularly rainy breaktime at school and it always made them laugh. They played a few rounds, and giggled a lot, trying to keep their voices down so they didn't wake up her brothers. But after round five, when Ezra had been thinking about whether to be a worm's bum or a giant's toenail for quite a while, Yasmin peered over at his sleeping bag and saw his eyes were closed. He was snoring very gently. Even Levi was already snoring next to her.

But Yasmin still couldn't stop wondering about whether her wish would be granted. Would Ezra be able to hear Levi? There was no way she was going to be able to fall asleep. She lay for a while with her eyes open, looking up at the glow-in-the-dark stars she'd stuck to her ceiling.

When it was just her and Levi sometimes she'd fallen asleep wondering if she'd wake up and everything would have been a dream. Sometimes she'd wanted that to happen. Everything would return to normal with no magic llamas, no speaking and no mayhem. But she didn't want that any more; she wanted to share her amazing llama secret. She wanted it to be real.

And it was . . .

Yasmin's eyes fluttered open to early-morning light. She'd managed to fall asleep but now there was something making a racket. What was that? It sounded like singing or maybe a radio.

Groggily she sat up in bed, yawning wide and pushing her unruly hair away from her face.

'What's that noise?' Ezra groaned, rolling over in his camp bed and putting his pillow over his head.

'I don't know,' Yasmin replied, her eyes barely open.

She rolled out of bed and followed the sound over to the window. Peering out, the sight she saw had her suddenly wide awake.

'Ezra, come here quick!'

Ezra rushed over and joined Yasmin. There on the roof opposite, standing loud and proud, was Levi singing at the top of his lungs.

'GOOOOOOOOOOOOOOOOOOOOOOOODD MOOOOOOOORNIIINGGGGG, SLEEPYHEADS!'

'AGGGHHHHH! LEVI, I CAN HEAR YOU!' Ezra yelled back.

'HE CAN HEAR YOU!' Yasmin yelled too.

'We can all hear you both! Shut it!' a neighbour shouted out of their window.

Yasmin, Ezra and Levi burst into fits of laughter.

Ezra turned to Yasmin, his hands over his ears. 'Gosh, he really is loud, isn't he?'

Yasmin smiled, big and wide. 'Yep, that's Levi.'